North Woods at Night

Literary Reflections on Maine's Largest Forest

Edited by Steven Long | Introduction by Ret Talbot

12 Willows Press
Winterport, Maine
www.12willowspress.com

FOREST
SOCIETY
of MAINE

Table of Contents

Acknowledgments

Some of the works in this collection were previously published in the following:

"After Dark or Taking After My Father" by Patricia Smith Ranzoni in her collection *ONLY HUMAN: Poems from the Atlantic Flyway* (Sheltering Pines Press, 2005)

"Black Powder Fire" by Patricia Smith Ranzoni in her collection *Hibernaculum & Other North-Natured Poems from Maine's Patricia Smith Ranzoni* (OneWater Press, 2010)

"Lunar Eclipse" by Bruce Pratt in the anthology *The Poeming Pigeon: Cosmos: A Literary Journal of Poetry* (Poetry Box, 2020)

"Man Climbing Katahdin" by William Carpenter in his collection *Rain* (Northeastern University Press, 1985)

Note: In Alice Bolstridge's "Moonlight on Snow," the line "I am become light and shadow" echoes the phrase "Now I am become Death, the Destroyer of Worlds," famously attributed to Robert Oppenheimer as he observed the Trinity nuclear test in July 1945. The original phrase comes from Krishna in the *Bhagavad Gita*: "I am Time, the powerful destroyer of worlds, grown immense here to annihilate these men."

Editor's Note
Steven Long

It's hard to fathom the scale of Maine's North Woods. Spanning 3.5 million acres, it is 1.5 times larger than Yellowstone and Grand Canyon National Parks combined. This rugged landscape—blanketed with trees, mosses, lichens, shrubs, grasses, ferns, and flowering plants—was sculpted thousands of years ago by the massive Laurentide Ice Sheet. As the glacier retreated, the land transformed into the vibrant forest we see today, teeming with diverse wildlife. Animals roam the dense woods, flourish in the lush, damp undergrowth, and glide through the trees, filling the air with life. Beneath the surface, fish dart through clear lakes and winding streams, completing the rich tapestry of this ecosystem.

Thirty-eight writers capture the magic that fills these woods after dark in *North Woods at Night: Literary Reflections on Maine's Largest Forest*. They transport us deep into the wilderness through poems, stories, and essays, where the familiar becomes mythical and nocturnal sounds echo across time. I hope this collection gives you a sense of the timeless beauty and mystery of the North Woods.

I want to extend my heartfelt thanks to Ret Talbot for his insightful introduction, which guides readers through timeless literary themes of woods at night, Annaliese Jakimides for her invaluable editorial assistance, Dan Kirchoff for creating a fantastic cover and map, and Mariella Travis for the brilliant book layout and overall design.

Proceeds from the sale of this anthology will support the Forest Society of Maine and its mission to conserve Maine's forest heritage for future generations.

Introduction
Ret Talbot

Rewilding the Woods at Night

"After thousands of years we're still strangers to darkness, fearful aliens in an enemy camp with our arms crossed over our chests."
—Annie Dillard

The essay I penned last year for *Rivers of Ink: Literary Reflections on the Penobscot*, this anthology's predecessor, was set in the Maine North Woods at night, which is the subject matter of this book. My narrative was grounded in a specific spot on a specific night when I heard the yelps of coyotes while contemplating the embers of a dying fire and the weight of history and its consequences. In my essay, the woods at night set the stage for reflective thought, as I pondered the necessity of seeking answers to modern problems in an ancient past. The actual night described in my essay transpired much the way I wrote it—on a canoe trip, by myself, in the shadow of Ktàtən—but, thinking back to the writing, the mechanics of it, I'm aware veracity is only part of the story. As writers, we are like builders. We decide what we want to build and then choose the tools best suited to our vision. I knew the narrative I wanted to tell. I chose the scene that I thought might best convey it: the North Woods at night.

The woods-at-night is an age-old literary trope, and, as you will discover in these pages, it's one we writers often find irresistible. In part, this is because the darkened forest can easily occupy both a literal and a symbolic space. It is also because, as a setting, a dark night in the woods does a lot of heavy lifting. In the space of a sentence ("She entered the forest on a moonless night"), the writer can transport the reader to a place that is both familiar and mysterious. Beautiful and menacing. Sedate and unsettling. A forest path at night can be an oddly familiar tract through a foreign landscape where anything can happen.

It's no wonder we have such a visceral reaction to a woods-at-night scene. Many of us grew up with warnings and admonitions, even if the woods in question were little more than a median between a divided highway, a local park, or a tract of disordered underbrush beneath a canopy of autumn leaves between neighbors' homes. "Don't go into the woods at night," seemed prudent, even if the actual threats remained elusive. From an early age, stories reinforced the advice. In fairy tales like *Little Red Riding Hood* and *Hansel and Gretel*, we were confronted with the harrowing thought of children alone in dark, dangerous woods. We encountered the shadowy wilds where Mole and Rat got lost and where a headless horseman rode along a forest track "thickly shaded by overhanging trees" and which "occasioned a fearful darkness at night."

By high school, we'd perhaps made an uneasy truce with the woods at night. We were maybe less afraid of the dark, and in time we found that dark woods were a place for us teenagers to engage in activities best hidden from the light. But then our teachers got involved. Many of this anthology's contributors (as well as many of its readers, no doubt) are students of literature and know that the woods-at-night trope is not limited to fairy tales. Pick up the oldest surviving piece of English literature, *Beowulf,* and you will find "wolf-inhabited slopes" and "savage fen-paths" of a secret land where "frost-bound" branches overhang a lake that burns with fire at night. In the opening of Dante's *Divine Comedy*, the narrator is "within a forest dark," the very thought of which "renews the fear." And don't forget how Shakespeare repeatedly returns to the woods at night—where outlaws lurk in *Two Gentlemen of Verona* and we feel the ominous dread in Macbeth's nocturnal meeting with the "secret, black, and midnight hags" who foretell of a deadly forest that will creep toward a bloody, nighttime battle.

In short, we were conditioned to see the woods at night in literature as more than a literal landscape. No longer did we experience it for the actual moonlight through a crown of trees, the authentic sound of the whippoorwill, or the honest shadow of a bat blinking out the stars. English teachers instructed us to ask, "What do the woods at night symbolize?" and we obediently plumbed the depths of the night for symbolic value and figurative meaning. We came to appreciate many of the authors of the so-called classics probably didn't intend for us to take the dark woods at face value. From Hawthorne to Conrad, Mary Shelley to Brontë, these prototypes of Western literature frequently return to what Shelley's Frankenstein calls "the miserable night" where the "cold stars shone in mockery, and the bare trees waved their branches above." It is where Frankenstein is driven to "fearful howlings," and while the visage is terrifying, we understand it is what the night represents that is the point.

"Mature" readers instinctually approach literary woods at night as Conrad's Marlow does. We "penetrated deeper and deeper into the heart of darkness," understanding we were confronting imperialism, savagery, and moral collapse just as much as "an impenetrable forest." We came upon the benighted Jamaican jungle in Jean Rhys's *Wide Sargasso Sea*, and we immediately understood Antoinette, the story's Creole protagonist, was up against a lot more than a dark forest without a flashlight. In entering the woods at night, Rhys signals an inward turning toward introspection, where the trauma of colonization collides with the sinfulness of slavery. "It is still night and I am walking towards the forest," Antoinette says, and we know the thin slippers and long dress she wears are not simply apparel. She is "sick with fear," as we are for her. Her madness, which will end on another night as she jumps from the roof of a sequestered English mansion engulfed by flame, emerges not from the night or the tangled wood but from her own identity slipping away into what that night represents. We are gut-punched that she makes no effort to save herself. "If anyone were to try to save me," she says, "I would refuse." Rhys knew the narrative she wished to build, and she skillfully uses the tools, including the woods at night, to construct it with heartbreaking precision and effect.

Not every nighttime woodland scene in literature is laden with doom and hidden meaning, though. Thoreau tells us, "Night is certainly more novel and less profane than day," and he describes a beautiful nighttime walk in the woods—what he calls "a very different season" with "the whole landscape ... more variegated and picturesque than by day." In *Their Eyes Were Watching God*, Hurston's protagonist Janie "felt like a child breaking rules" when she gleefully sets out into the midnight woods to go fishing. For Max, the woods at night become a magical place of discovery inhabited by Wild Things, and it is pleasant, albeit otherworldly, when Lucy first meets Mr. Tumnus "in the middle of a wood at night-time." Even Shakespeare gives us the enchanted nighttime forest in *A Midsummer Night's Dream*. But overall, in the literature we were assigned, the woods at night often signaled something foreboding and symbolic. And so, it was with this in mind that I first began reading *North Woods at Night: Literary Reflections on Maine's Largest Forest*.

I am pleased to say that the authors of these stories, essays, and poems have rewilded the literary night with narratives and visions that transcend tropes and honor the physical place that binds the pieces together. The Maine North Woods are an immense, difficult-to-define, and diverse landscape with an equally diverse cast of characters. On these pages, you will encounter the Woods through the lens of poetry and prose, but you will see it for only some of what it is. The North Woods is not a monolith that can be contained by a single anthology any more than it can be interpreted through any one storytelling tradition. I learned much about Maine through the writers to whom I was exposed in school and whom I choose to read today. Thoreau and Longfellow, Sarah Orne Jewett and Edna St. Vincent Millay, E. B. White, Richard Russo, Stephen King, Elizabeth Strout, Susan Conley, Rachel Carson, Bill Roorbach, Morgan Talty—I could go on, but instead I think it fitting to close with a thought from Talty.

Author of *Night of the Living Rez* and *Fire Exit*, Morgan Talty is a citizen of the Penobscot Indian Nation, who, according to the *New York Times*, "has assured himself a spot in the canon of great Native American literature." Considering this accolade, Talty quips, "Why isn't it simply the great American canon?" In an interview with *The Rumpus*, he asks, "Why are we constantly being compartmentalized?" His answer? "It's only categorized this way through the non-Native Western lens."

As we dive into these stories, keep in mind that Native stories about this place have existed since long before the first Europeans viewed North America, much less colonized it. Long before land was stolen. Long before attempts to eradicate culture. Long before cultural appropriation. These stories existed before *Beowulf* and the *Divine Comedy*. Before Shakespeare and Hawthorne wielded night as a literary tool. Western literary tropes emerged by looking at the world through a European lens, where the night was diminished with technology and the remaining darkness made wildlands a place to fear. We must remember this lens is a relatively new one for the North Woods, and, by itself, it's as insufficient as the artificial boundary placed around it. To the Wabanaki, to the four federally recognized Indigenous Nations living in what we call Maine, homeland is rooted in connection to land, not government. With this knowledge, I encourage writers and readers to recognize that when we write and read about this place, we are adding to the "American canon," which includes Native stories that inform a truth we all should seek.

With the above in mind, I am thrilled that proceeds from this anthology will be donated to the Forest Society of Maine, which seeks to be a conduit for relationship-building between Wabanaki communities and forest landowners. I believe the North Woods at night, as presented here, can add to a rich storytelling tradition and occupy both a literal and a symbolic space of community, compassion, and stewardship.

Map of the North Woods
Dan Kirchoff

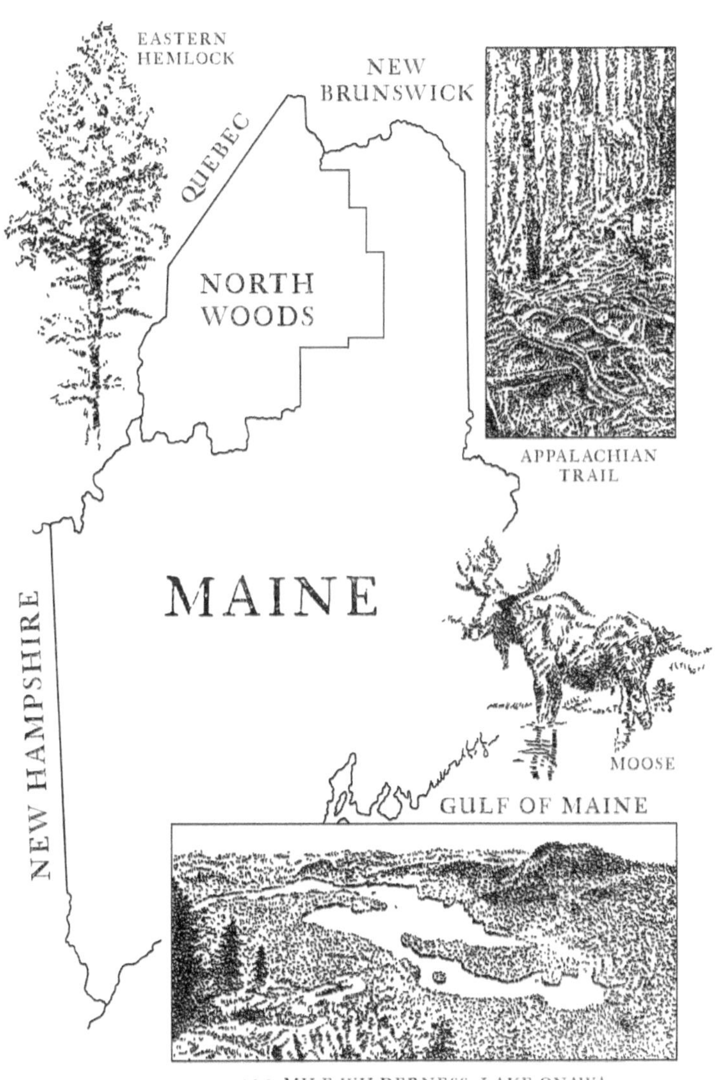

Log Drive, November 1976
Rick Doyle

Along the winding River Road, bending
left and right, white birches gleam
in darkness unrelieved by northern lights;
from the river below, as if in response,
starlight glimmers on the bark of spruce and balsam fir
drifting downstream in great black rafts.

The Wisps of the North Woods
Devin Gifford

The dark cloaks the wood
to sift out all but the brave.
Tree trunk golems guard the gate.
In their branches,
an owl's eye gleams.

To find the right slice of night,
listen for the space between the trees
that whispers in a language you've never spoken,
and hold your heart close to your chest,
lest it snag on your sleeve.

The owl, with its pivotal nod,
should let you pass.
Look the dark in its grinning face
until it winks and welcomes
the wisps.

Little drops of living starlight bob and dance.
Hold steady against their blaze.
And if you do catch one,
bottle it, sing to it, boil it for tea,
just keep its light far from your heart.
They feed on misery.

Night Out
Amy Ray

Tonight, we canoe out secretly, quietly, against camp rules. We whisper and stifle giggles. The paddles slice through the pewter depths below us, displacing billions of tiny diamonds. Stars, an impossible number of stars in all directions. The turtles do not bother to slip off the boulders tonight as we pass.

The few canvas tents behind us that are still lit glow like soft, dull-green lanterns. There is nothing to hear but a quiet sloshing as we separate the waters. One by one, we stop paddling and drift—three red canoes, six ten-year-old girls quieted. Not the raucous adventure we had planned.

At ten, we do not know how to discuss beauty. We do not have the words to say, yet we understand this is a significant moment. The power and enormity of this night will always be with us.

Seemingly all at once, without a word, we J-stroke and turn back toward shore. Drowsily and silently, we paddle side by side.

We are back in damp sleeping bags inside musty tents in time for bed check at midnight.

I drift off and dream we are swimming through a deep purple sky, flicking tiny stars in one another's hair above the black woods.

Two Nights, Two Flights
Matt Bernier

Little Brown Bat
One night, walking the dog under a full moon,
there's a graceful whir and swoop above me,
too late for chipping sparrows to be foraging,
Mercury like a warning light about to give up,

and I realize that a little brown bat has survived
its plague of white-nose syndrome brought here
by spelunkers, those who followed migrating bats
in and out of caves while crossing back and forth

from light to dark, warm to cold, living to dead,
misunderstanding bats' returns from hibernacula
as a resurrection that would faithfully reoccur,
not understanding what breaking that plane meant,

little brown bats now in a crisis of extinction,
so I'm honored by the bat killing mosquitoes
above me, flying below the radar and sharply
silhouetted in moonlight, echolocating all life.

Barred Owl
Out again in splendid darkness, Big Dipper emptying,
and I hear a barred owl hooting, loud and crazy,
as though demanding change from a quarter moon;
on the brim of summer and sounding like nesting season

in March all over again, and I wonder why the owl
feels like defending its territory of ancient white pines
when they're barely casting shadows in this dim light,
owl watching the meek run around a forest floor as

wind slowly brings change, clouds across the moon
and pine boughs lifting like the dark, sinewy arms of
massing protestors; barred owl predicting weather,
a depression, a pressure drop, hard rain a-coming.

midnight, daicey pond
faith lane

midnight
i wiggle out from beneath my quilt
slip on my sweater and crocs
head outside into the cold

after i've finished my business
i walk silently
in darkness
down to the dock
no flashlights for me
i have my phone if need be
that is to say ...
if someone else wanders this way
otherwise
darkness

and starlight
gazing up i greet old friends
orion, mighty hunter
queen cassiopeia
pegasus with the wilting andromeda

turning i locate the big dipper
ursa major
great bear, muin
little dipper is not visible here, now
i marvel at the sweep of spilled milk
that is our galaxy viewed sideways

all is so still
until a loon calls hauntingly for their mate
i shiver
thrilled
and turn to head for bed

Winterlude
Catherine J.S. Lee

It's all that's left now,
a broad and winding avenue
through the forest
on this long-abandoned estate
where an imposing lodge once stood.

Tonight, sharp with frost,
the gibbous moon shines down on fresh snow
that sparkles like crystals
even in this subdued light.
Our footsteps, his and mine,
are the first to pass this way,
the path unfurling ahead of us
in a wide and unmarked ribbon.
Balsams grow thickly here,
bearing their snowy burdens,
and the still air carries their bracing fragrance
of green wood and spicy resin.

Stars twinkle
in the high black stripe of sky
between the tall trees on either side,
Rigel and Betelgeuse and Sirius
vibrating in my imagination
with the music of the spheres.
A sudden wind rises and snow begins to swirl—
from the balsams,
from the spruces,
from the bare limbs of birch and maple,
as though constellations themselves are falling,
as though everything
is being sprinkled with stardust
like that from which our world was born.

The Dark Sky Zone
Nancy J. Hayden

John stoked the woodstove before dinner, and now, at 8 p.m., it had turned the well-insulated bunkhouse sleepy warm. Although tired from the five-hour drive north, we weren't quite ready to hit our bunk beds for the night. John signed up as the naturalist volunteer for a week in mid-February at the Appalachian Mountain Club's (AMC) Medawisla Lodge, located east of Kokadjo on Second Roach Pond. It's part of AMC's 100-Mile Wilderness and recently designated The Maine Woods International Dark Sky Park. I came along to experience the dark sky zone and a real winter in Maine's North Woods. It had been a mild winter here, too, with temperatures reaching fifty degrees a couple of days earlier, but by the time we arrived, it had turned cold again, and there was still plenty of snow cover.

John looked tired sitting on the bunkhouse couch. I knew he could fall asleep at this hour and be down for the night, but I knew I couldn't. I suggested a walk. As the designated nighttime dog walker at home, I enjoyed walking in the dark.

He sat up. "Great. Let's go."

We donned winter coats, boots with microspikes (it was quite icy in spots), a headlamp, hats, and scarves and mittens (the temperature had dropped into the teens) and headed out. The first few breaths of cold clean air revived us. We walked down the side of one of the cross-country ski trails, passing cabins and an occasional whiff of woodsmoke. The waxing crescent moon had already come and gone, but even without the moon, we didn't need the headlamp. The snow on the wide, well-groomed trail showed us the way.

After about a quarter mile, we turned off onto an ungroomed side trail that headed to the pond. Snowshoers had come this way during the thaw and now deep, frozen tracks turned the trail into a real ankle buster. I switched on the lamp as we trudged over the rough, icy snow. Birch and spruce trees closed in overhead, and with the narrow light of the headlamp, it felt like we were walking through a dark tunnel. Snowshoe hare tracks in the woods looked fresh, but we noticed no other signs of nighttime creatures. Just us.

A short distance later, the trail opened to the lake shore and the frozen lake beyond. They call it a pond, but it looked more like a lake to me. No houses or camps lined the edge of the water, only the thick, dark northern forest. Small spruce trees, stuck into the ice, marked the trail that crossed this side of the pond. Because of the earlier thaw, we'd checked with the lodge manager upon our arrival about the status of the ice. As long as we stayed on the trail, we were fine.

We turned off the headlamp and walked onto the lake. Silence surrounded us except for an occasional quiet groan, the sound of the frozen lake murmuring its secrets. We stared at the starry night sky. Thin clouds soon dissipated, and the stars became more intense. Jupiter shone bright, as did the constellations Orion, the Big Dipper, and Cassiopeia. John pointed out the North Star and the Pleiades.

The Milky Way, a silvery wispy cloud, curved across the sky. It had been a long time since I'd seen the Milky Way. Even in our sparsely populated Midcoast neighborhood, light pollution from streetlights, neighbors' floodlights and porch lights, car and truck lights, and even the sky glow from distant towns made it hard to see true darkness. Most people across the U.S. can't see a natural dark sky where they live. They've never seen the Milky Way in all its glory.

We stood still for a long time, tilting our heads back, knowing that at our age, this type of looking would probably give us a neck ache the next day, like warbler neck when birdwatching during spring migration. But still, we stared. We felt so small within this great starry universe. Is that why people have such a sense of wonder and awe at a brilliant night sky? Or is it because, as tiny as we are, we feel part of the vastness, the magnificent cosmic mystery that lets us leave behind, even if just for a moment, the individual self?

A shooting star flashed and disappeared.

John put his arm around me and squeezed. "My feet are cold."

So, we came back to ourselves and once more became just two old people standing on a frozen lake in the North Woods of Maine. And that was good, too.

Under the Wolf Moon

Todd McKinley

See here, the moonshadows falling on snow,
filling the path to the river's edge—

Watch how the darkness curls
under the crests of drifts sweeping
across this line I marked yesterday.

Trace these new tracks I stamp
to wander closer to the fox's cry,
his hoarse breath breaking twilight ...

Stand with me where the ice sheets buckle
on the bank: river-glass spreads wider,
an unbroken pane of blue-white
silvered under waning gibbous.
Star-glister cuts this twilight
like the cold—
this winter air sparks
revelations in snow-dust and ice-crystal.

Gather all of these elements
starshine and moonglow,
oak-shadow and boot-prints—
pour each one into yourself
settling into lungs and blood,
contraction and expansion flowing,
stirring cavities infant
and ancient
to the surface:

Be like the silhouette loping along this ice-road
leading toward the wolf moon:
my memory reaches for
the cry echoing in the woods.

January Nocturne
Garrett Conover

Of a winter night
when the moon is full
and cold holds stillness
like a brittle gem.
Light spills to river
with silver bright;
trees pop suddenly
in plunging frost,
their shadows black
upon brilliant snow.
There seems extra gravity
to such fullness,
no staying asleep
within friendly blankets,
shared heat of sweetheart
lying curved to snuggle
the warmest fit.
Something too compelling
afoot this night,
strong as unseen current
insistent under ice.
In sleep my loved one seems to know
that this must be
and does not wake when I slip away,
or stir to hear cold-snow squeak
beneath my snowshoes
taking flight.
And I am not alone
while my shadow prances,

a pair of fox tracks
merge and diverge,
printed fresh as mine.
They keep close to shore
to vanish and watch,
but not be seen.

Ravens are not sleeping either,
but stay talkative and restless.
They seem as curious as me,
with no resistance
to illuminated night.
When I imitate their calls
they check their flight
with a wind-ripping rush
to loop, and cock an eye
upon my strangeness
wandering the ice.
With abundant grace
my love does not stir
when I slip back in.
As if in dreaming she understands
this midnight gift is mine,
and does not wake enough
to wonder
what fantastic wings
called my snowshoes to whisper
beneath exquisite skies
where joyous breath hangs luminous
in lovely cold,
where night-talking ravens fly.

Telling the Forest from the Trees
Kathleen Ellis

1
The Great Northern Forest
remains to be seen.

2
From the air, the land below
begins and ends
in trees.

3
When the wind is howling,
we mistake it
for the trees.

4
Living. Breathing.
The essence of the forest.

5
Woods are what we call it
instead of Forest.
All twelve million acres.

6
Entering the canopy of trees,
undercover.

7
Look up   look all the way up
from the floor of the forest.

8
The first thing I noticed when I moved East
were the trees right up to the roadside,
thick and foreboding.

A hedge of sorts.

9
When we pulled over, I edged myself
into the trees, to know what it is
to surrender.

10
I had a mantra when I moved, borrowed
from Gary Snyder: *learn the plants,
learn the animals, learn the trees.*

11
I walk into your shadow, yours the same
as mine.

12
At night, we sleep under the hemlocks,
under cover of the boundless edge
of branches and stars.

The Gates of Hell Are South
Sherry Pineau Brown

There is no dark like Moosehead dark.

Growing up, I feared the dark at our family's camp. I often awoke in the middle of the night, confused as to where I was, and prayed that the urge in my bladder would go away so that I would not need to venture outside to use the outhouse. I'd hold my hand in front of my face, terrified because I couldn't see it, wiggling my fingers and touching my nose to be sure I still existed. Most often, I'd pull the sleeping bag over my head and try not to think about the creatures—both natural and unnatural—that lived in that dark on the northeastern-most tip of Moosehead Lake in Northeast Carry, Maine.

Thoreau referred to Northeast Carry, the traditional spot to portage canoes from the lake to the West Branch of the Penobscot River, as "a remarkable kind of light to steer for—daylight seen through a vista in the forest—but visible as far as an ordinary beacon at night." More than a beacon, my father and his brothers, who helped my grandfather—my Pépère—build the camp in the 1960s, have always referred to the place as "Heaven." Someone even made a hand-carved sign that now hangs in the front room to tell all who enter that "The Gates of Hell Are South"—a phrase referring to the gates travelers drive through to enter the North Maine Woods.

Like Heaven, the camp is difficult to get to. The trip from my father's mill town home of Jay to Greenville at the base of the lake is about one hundred miles or, to put it in Maine terms, a two-hour drive. From there, drivers choose between Rockwood on the west side of the lake, a bit longer, but with more tar roads, or Kokadjo on the east side. Both towns are about twenty miles north of Greenville, and both tend to be the last form of civilization (and indoor plumbing) travelers will see until they return from camp. From Kokadjo, camp is only about twenty-five miles, but can take anywhere from one to two hours to travel. The shale-covered roads twist through the North Woods, making them slow-going at best and tire-slicing at worst. It is not unusual to have to change and plug at least one tire during a visit. As children growing up in the 1970s and '80s, my siblings, cousins, and I often rode to camp in the bed of my father's mini Toyota pickup. The bed was covered by a cap that protected us from the thick dust kicked up on the journey north. As kids, we fought over who would get to sit on the wheel well, which we deemed as the prime seat. On the long drive north, my father slid open the back window every so often and yelled back to make sure we were still alive. It never occurred to us to be jealous of the dog who got to ride up front.

In Maine, people often refer to any house on a lake as a "camp"—even though most are second houses with all the comforts of home. Our camp, however, *is* a camp. Built to hold nearly a dozen men for deer or (for the ones lucky enough to win a permit) moose season. The original exterior of the place was covered in green tar paper and the interior walls still consist of exposed plywood. Water is pumped up from the lake by a hand pump, and twelve twin beds built from two-by-fours—six of which are bunk-bed style—fill three bedrooms and the main room. Nearby, an outhouse also serves as a shed for tools, gas, and the lawnmower. The outhouse at camp now, I must mention, is not the original. When I was three, Pépère died exiting the original, which I only learned from family stories years later. I always imagined that as he took his last breath, he slammed open the door, pants around his ankles, staring out at the lake and the Heaven he had built. On the day he died, Folsom's Air Service, typically used to fly hunters, fishermen, and adventurers into the North Maine Woods, served as coroner. What a sight it must have been as the seaplane landed in front of camp and floated up to the beach to carry him south one final time.

Our camp is "decorated" with mounted deer antlers from each of the brothers. Pictures of men in buffalo-plaid jackets and hats posing beside hanging carcasses line the walls. There is a camaraderie to the pictures—of knowing a thing and a place. The pièce de résistance is a framed cartoon poster print of a camp nearly identical to ours titled "4 A.M." A sign tells us this is the "Stump Sitters Hunting Camp." Two men are fast asleep, laying askew on bunks, mouths agape, clad only in red-union suits. One man is passed out in the clothes he wore the night before, with his head down on a kitchen table that is covered in empty beer mugs, coffee cups, and poker chips. Another is wide awake reading by flashlight under his covers. A third man is in boots and a union suit beside the woodstove, tending the fire and starting coffee. The last is outside, sitting in the outhouse, the door open, shivering from the freezing cold and staring at a skunk. A whitetail peeks in another window as the carcass of another hangs from a rack. Someone took a sharpie to the print and wrote the names of my father and his brothers beside each of the men in camp. Then, in the margin, anyone who has attended a hunt at camp has written their name in ink or in Sharpie. The list is long—with most of my family members and their friends listed.

My name is not there.

My parents divorced when I was five, and I spent most of my time with my mother. Growing up, my father would take my sister and me to camp during early June for salmon season or late July to fish for lake trout—togue—but we never took part in a family hunt. In my mind, I imagined it was because we were girls, but I have seen pictures of my younger female cousins and my half-sister donning hunter's orange and a rifle—so gender could not be the only answer. I imagine it had more to do with the divorce and the demons left in my father from the Vietnam War, which resulted in a tank injury that grew more painful by the year.

This past October, we brought my father to my home to die. Surrounded by my uncles and cousins, he lay in his hospice bed and listened as they shared stories of years at hunting camp. He hadn't visited camp for over a decade. The roads, he said, were too rough, and it took too long to recover. But I could tell that the stories brought him solace and eased the fear of what was to come. Before he died, I dreamed of buying a boat large enough to not agitate his injury so he would be able to visit camp at least once again.

We never got the chance.

Like so many, after college, I left home for wider spaces, but the pull of the lakes, forests, and people of my home was too strong, so I returned. I yearned, in part, to reconnect to places from my youth. After the birth of my daughter, I decided that camp would be one of those places, but our hunts, I knew, would be different. I also knew that summer, not the early spring or late fall, would be our time at camp. Our time would be about swimming and paddling. Nothing that would add our names to the "Stump Sitters Hunter Camp" print.

And yet, on each visit, as evening approached, dinner was cleared, and the sun started its descent over the lake, it was time.

"Everyone in the car. Time for the Moose Hunt!"

I'd drop the back seat of the SUV, and whichever kids were with us would pile in with pillows, blankets, bags of chips, boxes of cookies, handfuls of candy bars, and generally any other snack that they were never allowed to eat at home. As my father always said, "This is camp, you get to do whatever you want at camp!" We also ignored the rules of the road—four adults and three children in a five-seat SUV? No problem. Not enough seatbelts? Who needs seatbelts? You get to do whatever you want at camp! We'd then drive the dirt roads looking for the elusive Maine moose. Sometimes, we'd find one; sometimes, we'd find something else.

I remember one summer when friends and their kids were up for the week, and as we usually did, we piled into the SUV for our jaunt. We turned right out of the driveway and headed south alongside the lake. The dirt road was rough. At times, the ruts in the road and potholes filled with jagged stone were too much for our tires to handle, and we had to back up slowly until we found a place to turn around. I would close my eyes and pray that the tall grass we were backing into didn't hide a drop-off. As I peered into the thick undergrowth for any signs of an animal, I thought about my father and his brothers scouring these woods for animals.

We were the only ones on the road as we drove deeper into the North Woods. As night crept closer, I had to push aside the feeling of déjà vu—I swear this was the beginning of some horror movie.

"Okay, everyone quiet! I've seen deer on this ridge coming up a lot of times. Let's see if they're here now."

"Why do we have to stay quiet? We are in the car. Seriously, Mom."

The other two tweens laughed at my daughter's sass.

"If you're too loud, they can hear you through the car."

"Whatever," she said, rolling her eyes while taking a swig from a usually forbidden soda.

Almost instantly, the sky turned that dusky, dimmed light between day and night. This hunt was turning into a bust. I peered intently into the trees on the side of the road, hoping to see something staring back out at me. I took a sharp breath at a dark, hulky shape—could that be the body of a grazing moose? I looked harder. Nope. A stump. My eyes and brain tried to readjust. Hadn't it moved? I had done these hunts enough times to know that this time of the early evening wreaked havoc on the imagination. Every rock was a rabbit, every downed tree a moose or a bear. It was guaranteed that during every one of these hunts, some child or adult would point into the deep trees and yell, "Look, a moose!" only to discover that it was a blown-over tree.

The dark was on us now. We turned around and headed back. As we drew closer to the camp, I felt more and more defeated. The forty-five-minute hunt count consisted only of one rabbit, a few crows, and a chipmunk. We never saw a deer or a moose. While the rabbit resulted in an audible "Awwwwww" from the back of the SUV, none of the animals left any sort of lasting impression on our hunting party. This hunt was just a drive that could have happened anywhere.

"Hey, what is that?" my friend asked, pointing up to the top of a tree. I stopped the car and looked up.

Two glowing eyes stared down from a branch.

"I don't know, but it's big—what is that?"

I loved birds—especially birds of prey—hawks, eagles, osprey, and kestrels—something about the way they glided and swooped.

Almost as though on cue, the giant let out the telltale "Hoo, hoo, hoo."

One of the kids yelled from the back, "An owl! It's an owl! Cool!"

One of the other kids responded back with a "Hoo, hoo, hoo."

"I've never seen one this close," I said in awe.

The dark outline of the bird was massive, a prescient being welcoming the night. For what seemed longer than the minute it actually was, everyone in the car stared in silence. As if on cue, the owl dropped from the tree, swooped over the hood and the windshield, and flew into the darkness behind us. I watched in the rearview mirror as the night swallowed the bird.

"Wow," my friend replied after a moment of silence went through the car.

Back at camp, as we brought in all of our hunting gear (and snack wrappers), I looked up to see the stars beginning to salt the sky. I hoped the kids would settle in soon so the adults could enjoy some silence outside. After a few rounds of cribbage, the kids shuffled off to their beds with glow sticks and books, and the adults went outside to enjoy the darkness.

When at camp, looking up at the night sky is always a dizzying experience. It is difficult to take in the entirety of it—the jeweled sky seemed closer and more expansive than the sky at home. The slivered moon this night made the Milky Way look like the brush strokes of a Van Gogh painting. Silently, we sat atop the picnic table on the beach and listened as the lake lapped the pebbled shore in a rhythmic calm.

I looked up and gasped as a streak of light painted the inky night sky.

"Look! A shooting star. Make a wish!"

And then, as if on cue, there was another and then another. Soon, the sky was filled with lines of light. We all breathed in the beauty of it. It occurred to me that generations have seen these meteors hurtle from the Perseus constellation to Earth. Perhaps my father had sat on this beach and looked up and felt the same reverence, the same wonder. While my brain knew that the light meant that the meteors were dying, burning up in the Earth's atmosphere, some other part of me saw them as a gift of this place. Almost as though heaven itself was opening up and showering us with light from its core. I had never felt so connected to a place as I did at that moment.

Later, when I could no longer keep my eyes open, I pulled the sleeping bag over my head—not in fear, but in a contentment that can only come from understanding one's place in the world. Perhaps tomorrow I will add my name to the margins of the print. Perhaps tomorrow we will find a moose.

Night Vision

Sarah Carlson

We bundle up,
climb aboard,
slide into the night.
Rocky shore recedes
as we make our way slowly
to the middle of the lake.
Once there
we cut the motor,
snuggle in, and look to the sky.
There is no wind,
so we drift at the whim
of the waters that hold us afloat.
I seem to remember
we were hoping to see
a satellite of some sort,
and that perhaps we even did.
But the deeper memory
is how astounding it was
to sit and look,
wait and allow our beings
to adjust.
Loon calls echo,
our breathing slows,
our bodies relax.
A few stars at first,
then more
        and more
                and more.

Constellations appear,
our galaxy seems to blossom
in a sky that,
though very dark,
has tones and shades and nuances.
We speak in whispers
messages of love and gratitude
for each other,
for these moments that
fill us with wonder
at how night vision
brings so very much
into focus.

Black Powder Fire
Patricia Smith Ranzoni

night coat
she goes out

dark as bark
hood to ground

no one on earth
knows where she is
but the dawn ones

lifts her nostrils
to sense what else
is about   where

circles the lake
in first snow slush
rubbing as she goes

spruce
        fir
        ash

shushsh
        shushsh

ink drops off the alders
locate her face
but she is but a flow
through
the waking woods

    invisible

a hunter might
take her
for a lucky bear

want her
    load his muzzle
    shatter her heart

Moonlight on Snow
Alice Bolstridge

March 1997, a full-moon night
snowshoeing through the north woods
on a trail west of Haystack Mountain,
I admire the play of shadows
and light scattering sparkles on the snow,
until I come to an opening, and I look up
to see the comet Hale Bopp shine
over the bald snow-cap of the mountain.
As far away as that comet is,
I am touched all through by it.
What does it mean, this thrill
of being in wild woods and viewing
the motion and reflected light
of mere rock and ice? I am lost.
I am become light and shadow,
each tiny sparkle on the snow, a tree,
solid rock. I am become a wedding
of consciousness and matter streaking
through space and time, trailing clouds
of dust, debris, and vapor millions of miles
behind. Shades of Wordsworth, "Trailing
clouds of glory do we come." And go.
I am made of the same elements as trees,
light and shadow, Hale Bopp, starshine
on snow—dumb atoms that always were
and always will be, eternally transforming,
as wild and unreasoning as the rabbit
 leaving tracks in the snow.

100 Miles
Greg Westrich

A little more than an hour ago, my wife, Betsy, and our dog Moxie had dropped me off where the Appalachian Trail (AT) crosses Maine Route 15 a few miles north of Monson: the beginning of the 100-Mile "Wilderness." I always thought of it in quotation marks because the trail didn't go through actual wilderness. Hikers gave the section that name because it was the longest section on the whole AT without a town or paved road crossing.

Before entering the woods, I had read the warning sign next to the trail:

CAUTION

There are no places to obtain
supplies or help until you reach
Abol Bridge—90 miles north.
You should not attempt this section
unless you carry a minimum of ten
days' supplies. Do not underestimate
the difficulty of this section.
Good hiking!

I walked past the sign and into the woods through an arch of dark, overhanging branches. Betsy would meet me at Abol Bridge in six days, ninety-three trail miles from where I stood.

Leeman Brook crashed through a narrow canyon one hundred feet in front of the shelter. Moments ago, I had climbed down the slick, black rock into the gorge, stepped across the stream, and then climbed thirty vertical feet to reach the shelter. Between the shelter and the gorge, the ground was a level sheet of bare, black slate. Staring at the expanse of slate was vertigo-inducing; it seemed to be moving slightly. It took me a few moments to realize that the clouds were reflected on its surface—it was their movement I saw. The rock felt warm, so I lay on my back and looked up through the trees to the drifting clouds as I ate my cheese and apple. My muscles felt loose and relaxed for a change. It always amazed me how quickly the problems and stresses of daily life melted away on the trail.

After my snack, I walked the three miles to Little Wilson Falls—the highest on the whole AT. The falls dropped down a hundred-foot slate cliff into a black canyon. Cedar trees grew on the ledges and down from the top of the canyon in snaky curves, reaching out into the mist from the falls. The stream passed through a narrow gateway to the right and disappeared between sheer black walls. I ate my lunch, listening to the falls and watching the shifting shadows deep within the canyon. No other hikers broke my solitude, surprising for such a warm June day. With one foot back at home being husband and dad, I still didn't feel completely at home in the woods.

The rest of the day, I hiked through several stream valleys. The streams were cold and swift, swollen with melted snow. I crossed them by leaping from rock to rock, using my hiking poles for balance. The ridges were open ledges with views of Borestone Mountain and the Bodfish Plantation. Dirty patches of snow hid in the corners of the rocky downslopes. Ravens soared on thermals, cawing at one another. I didn't see another hiker all day. I began to feel civilization sloughing off me like accumulated mud on my shoes or a snake shedding its skin.

I pushed on into the late afternoon, reaching the Long Pond Stream shelter around seven. I unpacked my gear and put on some water to boil for dinner. I laid my sleeping pad and bag out on the far right of the shelter, expecting other hikers for the night. Eating my noodles with a pouch of chicken in the growing gloom, I wondered how it was that I was still alone. In all of my years of camping and backpacking, I'd rarely slept out alone. In fact, I had hesitated to go for a multiday hike by myself, but in the end, I convinced myself that sleeping out alone was better than being a bear at home. On more than one occasion, Betsy had pointed out that I turned inward the more I missed time in the woods.

I climbed into my sleeping bag as night's darkness, slithering through the woods and out of the valley, overtook the shelter. The day's sounds were replaced by deeper, more mysterious goings-on. Two trees rubbed together in the breeze that whispered through the treetops, creating an irregular squeaking. I set my journal aside, turned my headlamp off, and burrowed deeper into my sleeping bag. I felt like I was a child again, listening to our old house settle, unable to relax enough to sleep. It seemed kind of silly, but every rustle and every crash in the woods made my heart skip a beat. There is a very real vulnerability in having to shed one's skin.

After a restless night, I awoke to the misty twilight of a cool dawn. The yellow sunlight pushed the darkness and all its creatures back into hiding. I ate a bagel smeared with peanut butter as I packed my gear, feeling a bit self-conscious about last night's uneasiness. Even so, as I slowly made my way up Barren Mountain, letting my sore muscles get back in the habit of walking again, I was dogged by the feeling that last night's darkness was following me. The spring wildflowers were beginning to bloom: small white bunchberries and foam flowers among the leaf litter, trout lilies in the sunny spots. Many of the trees were not fully leafed out, making the mountainsides a patchwork of green hues. Everywhere, luxuriant green mosses grew, and songbirds darted after insects or defended their corner of the world. Just beyond and beneath, spring shadows shifted and stalked the day.

I ate lunch on a rock near the birch-covered summit of Third Mountain. As I ate and aired out my feet and boots, a Canada jay jumped silently from tree to tree, getting closer and closer, its wings barely whispering. The bird had a gray back and wings; its shoulders and face were bright white. It had a black hood that ran from one black eye to the other around its head. I set a small piece of sausage on a rock a few feet from where I sat. After eyeing the morsel for a moment, the jay coasted down to the rock, grabbed the food, and retreated to a nearby tree to eat. When it was gone, he cocked his head and peered at me. I assumed it wanted more, but I realized that it had a message for me.

"You pale people are convinced time is a straight line that moves only in one direction," it seemed to be saying. "But time is a hoop of day and night bound together by shadow," it continued—or so I imagined.

I held out my hand, palm up, with another piece of sausage. With little hesitation, the jay swooped down and landed on my fingers. It snatched up the food and returned to the same branch and gulped it down.

"If you look into the shadows, you will know this is true," it continued. I started to respond but had nothing to say. The jay opened its wings and lifted silently from its perch. "But if you only live in the shadows, you will be lost and never return home."

Later, approaching West Chairback Pond to fill my water bottles, I spooked a young bull moose. He splashed out of the pond and into the woods. It always amazed me how such a large animal could disappear so easily into the trees without a trace. Back into the darkness's embrace. The only evidence that the moose had been there was some cloudiness in the pond where he was feeding.

I stopped where the side trail dropped down to East Chairback Pond. It was a beautiful campsite and a good place to see moose in the morning, but there was no shelter. To save weight, I didn't bring a tent. I needed to choose between camping under the stars or hiking another eight miles to a shelter. Realizing I wouldn't reach the shelter before nightfall and having already walked over fifteen miles, I decided to head down toward the water.

A few yards above the rocky shore of the pond was a large oak tree with a hawks' nest high in its branches. The ground beneath the tree was soft and level. I laid out my sleeping pad and bag, leaning my pack against the tree truck. While I made dinner, the shadow of Chairback Mountain crept toward me across the water; the female hawk sat in her nest, chatting with her mate as he came and went. Eventually, the shadow reached the oak tree, and the hawks settled in for the night, still occasionally murmuring to one another. After dipping my water bottles in the pond and letting them quietly fill, I readied for bed. I hung my shorts and socks on a nearby beech sapling and slid into my sleeping bag, making a pillow out of my fleece jacket. I set my headlamp and glasses against the tree trunk, just within reach. I closed my eyes and thought about the day's hike, trying to ignore the various sounds coming to me out of the dark. I still had not seen anyone in my two days on the trail.

I awoke, alert, heart pounding, but without knowing what had pulled me from my sleep. I lay there listening to the creaks and rustles of the night, feeling my dog Moxie asleep against my left side. Reaching out of the sleeping bag, I stroked her soft fur and drifted back to sleep with my hand resting on her shoulder.

The morning was cool; fog hung over the pond and wisps of the memory of Moxie beside me collected behind my eyes. I was alone. No dog.

A hundred yards down the shore, a cow moose and her calf stood knee-deep in the water, eating weeds from the muddy bottom. I sat on a rock and ate a peanut-buttered bagel. There was at least one other moose in the pond. Without my binoculars, it was hard to tell big rocks from moose at a distance. I watched for movement, but the wisps of fog in the angled, morning sunlight made every surface dance and slide around—as if the world was reorganizing itself a few degrees to the left of yesterday.

From East Chairback Pond, the trail dropped steeply down toward the Pleasant River through towering firs. I was sweating by the time I reached the road along the river. The trail crossed the road and followed the river toward where day hikers parked to head out to Gulf Hagas. The parking lot was empty; the morning was still and quiet. The river rushed around the rocks; a stand of old-growth white pines stood silently across the river. The trail curved around the pines and followed the river upstream toward Gulf Hagas. Most summer days, there would be dozens of hikers here having just forded the cold stream or preparing to. Today, it was silent; the shadowed path beneath the trees was inches deep in rust-colored needles. Even the sound of my footsteps was hushed. I decided to stop for a snack, less from hunger than from the hope that another hiker would happen along and break the spell of my solitude. Among the pines, I felt the cool shadows slipping around me.

Snack over, I continued toward White Cap Mountain. At Gulf Hagas Brook, the trail turned right and began to climb. It felt good to work my muscles. Once I got into a rhythm, the miles sailed by. On this south-facing slope, spring was further along: more flowers, more birds. As I climbed out of the hardwood forest and into the spruce and fir, there were fewer flowers and birds—although I did flush a spruce grouse. I stopped at the Sidney Tappen campsite to get water from the spring. Because the spring was down a steep side trail, I removed my pack and descended the stone steps with only my water bottles. The spring was nestled among granite boulders and shadows.

As I sat filling my bottle with the achingly cold water in the little pool at the base of a granite boulder, Betsy sat nearby.

"Trail water is the best," she said.

"Crisp. Like an apple," I replied. "You almost need to chew it. But it makes my teeth hurt."

"Life distilled down to the bare essentials: walking, water, simple food, and the woods."

"Yeah. This morning, I hit my stride. I've become one with it."

Betsy nodded; she felt it, too. It'd been a challenge, with the stresses of raising kids and working, to get here. I filled the second water bottle.

"Let's go eat," I suggested. But I was alone again.

The next few days passed in a blur of clear blue lakes, granite mountaintops, and deep, black nights in shelters surrounded by forests full of groans and creaks like distant voices. A muddy trail through a remote forest, newly awakened to the warming year, connected the nights. The darkness followed me, sliding in and out of dappled light beneath the emerging canopy. It rustled leaves, broke branches, and made inexplicable noises as it moved just beyond my vision.

I knelt on the coarse sand along the shore of Nahmakanta Lake, scooping out a small basin where the spring water bubbled up through the beach. The water filled the depression, and, after a moment, ran clear.

My son Henry and I lay on our bellies and noisily drank the cold water.

"Dad, if I close my eyes, I feel like I'm flying over the lake."

I lifted my face from the water and turned to see no one beside me.

Sometime later, I came to where Rainbow Stream drops through a stand of old-growth red pines. Looking up a hundred feet to the tops of the trees, my feet cushioned by a brown carpet of needles, I almost cried for the beauty of it—until my mom emerged from the shadows to hand me lunch.

Less than three miles from Abol Bridge, I stood on a dark, round boulder in the middle of Hurd Brook. The heavy forest around me seemed primordial in its decay. Every surface was covered with lichen or moss. The understory consisted almost entirely of fallen, rotting snags. A place where daylight never quite penetrated. The clear water sluiced around the boulders in the stream, racing toward the Penobscot River.

My daughter stood on a rock near mine. She lifted one leg and balanced on the other, her arms outstretched. "Look, Daddy, one leg." Her pink shorts were the only color among the rocks and dead trees.

I practically ran the last four miles north to the Golden Road and Abol Bridge. Six days in the wilderness and I felt more connected to the shadows than to the world beyond the woods. It felt natural that my mom would be miles from the nearest road and states away from her home with my lunch. And that my daughter would be standing on a boulder in deep woods that the sun never seemed to penetrate. Reality and imagination were interchangeable. My world had been reduced to walking, drinking water, eating food, and inhabiting shadows. I knew if I didn't get to the end of my hike soon, I never would.

Coming out of the woods was like walking through a door and into a daylight world of light and color, where dust from the road drowned the darkness and sent the shadows into hiding. A loaded logging truck rumbled by and sang across Abol Bridge's steel decking. I looked behind me and saw the shadows crouching beneath the trees. I walked across the bridge to where Betsy was parked, wisps of shadow clinging to my ankles and pack.

Growth Curve
Lee Sands

Out of darkness
    Into darkness
  From warm, wet womb
To cold, wet loam
Calfling moose emerges
  Out of one dark world
  into another
Through doorway marked by dusk,
 Warm brown softness,
 Gentle greeting,
 Familiar musk
*

Within branching,
Sweet, dark boughs
of downed evergreen embrace,
on bed of lichen & sphagnum,
Secluded, safe,
  Calf learns first—
Milk / Mother
Cold / Moon
Sleep
  While
Snowfall
Muffles
  Whole universe
*

Strengthening newborn legs,
Finding food & staying safe:
  Priorities, first days.

Most precious
        & yet
Somebody's would-be prey.
Mama dictates: *predators*; EVADE.

Crunch
        Slow
Ski-pole limbs striate snow
Indistinguishable from tree-trunk shadows
        Alternating
Lean black stripes / glare-white snow

Mama shows   way to go
        Slow
Through late season squall
        to something flowing—
Stone-stepping
Over stars reflected, seemingly
Glowing skyward from the riverbed
        Soon
Hooves stuck fast in muck—
        Breakfasting
Among frost-footed ducks
*

Down, around wooded bend,
Single hoof-tracks in snow
        Deceive—
Silently
A second set lifts,
Pauses in steamy breath &
Steps directly into the first
Forming   single file
Leading from forest

Dark mound & smaller mound

Stagger south to still,
Black river saltlick
        Where things move   quick
Calf learns
*

Turning,
        Greening,
        Warming,
Year weaves
Winter into Spring
&
Spruce saplings shoot—
        Grow sunward
Alongside calfling moose

Cow teaches calf
        Willow, aspen, maple, birch,
        Pin cherry, mountain ash, balsam fir

        Further
Turning,
        Browning,
        Greening,
        Weaving,

Calf soon feels new pressure of
        Antlers developing
Feels
        Pull outward
        Toward uncharted borders
*

Over pondweed, one
Blue-black morning,
Riverbank opposite reflects

Velvet, wide-racked, eclipsing shadow
At once   unfamiliar and instinctively known—
        Bull Moose
Descendant of giants
        Another
Black-bellied bark-stripper,
Crepuscular creature
Of shade and shadow,
        Another
Ink-eyed wanderer
Of in-between worlds

At a distance, in an instant, all
Steam-snort huff & thick musk &
        Thrash away
        Could have been a
Lucid dream amidst the rising
Morning dew

Yearling feels world anew
Knows what he must,
        Feels wild's pull
        & follows

The Ghost's Lament
Michelle Menting

Was it last spring in our woods when we found that shell
of toilet with its lid half-cracked, the bowl mid-surfacing
in leaves and mud? When you said, that bowl knew dolls,
knew turtles, knew happiness? I never did ask you to explain.

Last night I was lost out there or found myself again
looking down at that hole of chipped porcelain and leaves.
Moss had grown over the lip of the lid, something you said
wouldn't happen, that if left twenty years the white might gray,

perhaps even yellow, but nature wouldn't lay carpet
over the whole. But remember how the velvet of moss
clung to the trunk of hemlock and how you said it looked
like a green shrug on the body snug in its casket?

I never asked you to explain. Instead, I stood and watched
as you stripped lichen from a birch—also yellow, also
dying. And then last night, with only the moon slitting through,
I spotted again that patch of bare tree. I didn't think

there'd be a mark. But there in that cluster of fir and oak,
that birch shined like a glow-stick misplaced at a party
for lumberjacks. You should have seen it. But you weren't there.
I was walking on my own. I lost time. I lost place.

I found myself, there again, near the moss-covered porcelain.
I didn't wear a sweater. I no longer wear a sweater. I didn't
need bug spray. They no longer seem to bite. Later last night,
I moved to explore the stream dammed by beavers. They'd left,

you'd said, years ago, first one then the other, by trap
or disease. Did I ever ask you to explain? I only remember
how you sat on that bank, how you split a sandwich, cut it
in two, and watched those creatures swim below and resurface.

Up and again, up again. You'd watch them tote twig by twig
as they built their house, as they tried to stop the river
from rushing on through, from taking away their everything.
I wish I could tell you how those beavers remain. Somehow

they're still there. I wish I could explain. How every night,
beneath the same moon, I can watch them. How every night
we submerge, and we resurface.

Mrs. Jacobs and the Nuclear Winter
Nomar Slevik

The city of Caribou is about fourteen miles north of Presque Isle and serves as the geographical heart of Aroostook County. As the second-largest city in northern Maine (Presque Isle being the first), Caribou traces its origins to 1824, when it was initially settled. Originally known as Lyndon, the city attained incorporation in 1859 and underwent a renaming a decade later, adopting the moniker "Caribou" in homage to the abundant woodland creatures that once thrived in the region.

While Maine enjoyed large populations of caribou until the late 1800s, game hunters from across the country flocked to the state and nearly eradicated the species. Eventually, the state made hunting caribou illegal. There were reports of a small herd of caribou in the Katahdin region until 1914. Repopulation efforts were made in 1963 and again in 1993, but according to Matthew LaRoche, the superintendent of the Allagash Wilderness Waterway, the "reintroduction programs failed miserably." It is thought that most of them were killed by bears or coyotes in 1963, and the 1993 herd, outfitted with radio collars, either died or left the area.

Back in 1955, with herds still roaming, something else made its way into northern Maine.

It's late. Outside, in the deep darkness of a winter's night in a landscape vast and empty, the temperature is dipping well below zero and the first quarter moon is a sliver in the stillness of the heavens. You look at the calendar from Pat's Sunoco on the wall by the phone. It's only four days until Christmas, 1955. As you check your front door lock and turn to make your way up the stairs to bed, you notice something odd, something out of place, a color and a glow that should not be there, growing in the distance. You turn to study it, wondering if a neighbor's house or farm is aflame, but you immediately dismiss that idea. Whatever it is, it's getting brighter, and, yes, it must be getting closer as well. And now you want to go awaken your husband, but you're afraid if you look away, it will be gone. Then you know that you can't look away because in some way you cannot explain; you understand in a bone-deep way that the light, or whatever is within the light, is looking at you, too. Your name is Roberta Jacobs, and this night, you've been chosen to witness something few others in northern Maine, or the world, for that matter, have ever seen, something that would haunt you for the rest of your days.

That beautiful piece of writing is from the *Strange New England* podcast, which delightfully tells the tale of Mrs. Roberta Jacobs. Her sighting occurred on December 21, 1955, and I first came across her encounter from a Project Blue Book report sometime in the mid-aughts. The writing she submitted to the U.S. Air Force was every bit as beautifully detailed as the podcast.

Her property sat just off the tree line of the North Woods where she lived with her husband. He had drifted off to sleep long before she had finished her nightly cup of tea. As he slept upstairs, she placed the empty cup in the sink and exited the kitchen when something outside caught her eye. She wrote, in part:

I just turned out my kitchen light to go to bed. I saw this red glare. I thought it was a fire on the Washburn Road. So, I thought I would wait and see if I could see the flames; I'd know just about where it was. Then it got brighter and brighter, so bright it just couldn't seem to get any brighter, and then it just came right out of the sky. It either came from behind a cloud, or the light was so bright it showed miles ahead of the ship. The light was so bright it would [have] shown through the blackest cloud anyway. Well, I just stood there stunned; I couldn't believe my eyes. I thought they were playing tricks on me. I could see the flat bottom part going round and round really fast. Almost too fast for the eyes to see it. I thought it was a spaceship.

She may have been right.

She began to experience a presence from within the light. It was a confusing, emetic feeling. She continued, "I just can't explain it on paper, but there was life there, I'm certain. Nothing human, but alive." She did not see humanoid forms, but there were intelligent movements. "Like hurried movements," she explained:

> Not one, but many things. I say not human because whatever it was has made me sick in the pit of my stomach, and now, if I look where I saw it or picture it in my mind (that hurried movement), I get so nauseated. I know it will sound crazy to you, but it's the truth. And whatever it was, I'm sure they saw me when I moved, and I felt as though they knew just what I was thinking. I felt as though they had a telescope or something pointed at me.

The night sky was possessed by entities, and their haunted vessel glowed red and gold. At the bottom of the radiant aura was a spinning disc that hovered silently above her barn.

Roberta was scared, and she wanted to wake her husband. While the comfort of his presence was welcomed, she also wanted him to witness the oddity. She wanted to make sure she wasn't the only one who saw it. She wrote:

> I hollered for him to come down, never taking my eyes off it. I was sure it was going to disappear before he saw it. But when he was halfway down our stairs, the bottom part stopped going around—it speeded up so fast that it looked stopped to my eyes. Freddie came; I can't say he was very much awake; he's so hard to wake up suddenly like that. He took one look at it and said it was the moon. Then I took my eyes from it to look at him;

I said, just like this, "Are you crazy? Where did you ever see a
moon like that?" He then went back to bed.

The moon was in a waxing crescent that evening and would seem unable to
produce the brilliant light that she observed.

After Freddie dismissed the sighting and went back to bed, Roberta wanted
to call the authorities. Perhaps the nearby air force station could tell her what
occupied the sky above her property. As if reading her thoughts, which she already
sensed was possible, the craft vanished from sight. She further stated:

> I watched it disappear just exactly like it came. I had that feeling
> I told you of. I just knew *they*, or *it,* knew what I was thinking ...
> I mean, I could feel them, and it made me so nauseated. After I
> felt that they saw me, I was thinking, "Should I call the base?"
> And they just seemed to hurry so fast to get out of there. And
> then it disappeared just like it came.

The next day, she went out to the yard to see if there was any evidence of the oddity
having been there. She noticed a fresh stream of frozen water on top of the snow
near the barn. This was a curious find, as it had been too cold for any melting
to occur, and she surmised that the heat of whatever occupied her airspace had
caused the premature thaw.

She agonized over contacting the air force during the following weeks and
months. Her thoughts were consumed with the encounter, and, after finally
reaching a breaking point in February 1956, she contacted the local base. They
referred her inquiry to Project Blue Book, an organization within the air force
that responded to claims of UFO activity. They mailed her the typical anomalous
sighting form and questionnaire, and Roberta filled out everything thoughtfully
and with as much detail as she could remember. She mailed it back, hopeful that
someone could tell her what it was or, at the very least, tell her that she wasn't
crazy. No one from the organization contacted her. Project Blue Book closed
her case as "unknown" without an interview or any follow-up. I have personally
read numerous reports where an air force representative would either travel to
the witness's home or at least phone them for an interview. Why this wasn't done
in Roberta's case remains unknown.

A curious point raised by the *Strange New England* podcast was of the nuclear weapons that were stored near Caribou and during the very same time frame as Roberta's encounter. The Caribou Air Force Station, located just ten miles from her home, has an interesting history. According to the *Strange New England* podcast:

> [I]t was technically not run by the Air Force at all but by the United States Atomic Energy Commission from 1951 to 1962, when it was absorbed into the new Loring Air Force Base. Before it was called the Caribou Air Force Station, it was one of several secret bases run by the government; called the North River Depot, it was allegedly constructed for the storage, assembly, and testing of atomic weapons, the first ever constructed in the continental United States, built to house the growing nuclear stockpile of the nation. On that base stood [twenty-seven] vaulted concrete storage structures called igloos [which housed] conventional and nuclear weapons that sat in the middle of a great forest. It was America's first organized armory of nuclear weapons, the first on Earth.

Researchers of extraterrestrial activity have found numerous correlations between UFO sightings and nuclear sites. Could that have been why Roberta's visitor was in the area? At first glance, it would appear that Project Blue Book missed an opportunity to investigate the incident further by not pursuing additional inquiries with Roberta. But what if this was intentional? One might consider the possibility of a deliberate choice. Is it conceivable that the organization, along with the Caribou Air Force Station and other government entities, was already aware of extraterrestrial interest in nuclear technology? Robert Hastings, in his book *UFOs and Nukes,* said of this possibility, "Air Force, FBI, and CIA files declassified via the Freedom of Information Act establish a convincing, ongoing pattern of UFO activity at U.S. nuclear weapons sites extending back to December 1948." Public acknowledgment of purported UFO encounters and cover-ups involving air force bases and military facilities is steadily gaining acceptance, particularly with the recent surge in mainstream media coverage.

The last portion of the questionnaire asked, "In your opinion, what do you think the object was, and what might have caused it?" Roberta answered, "A spaceship. I'm certain it wasn't anything we have on Earth. But it was an airship; I'm sure of that. It was beautiful, just beautiful. There is really no word [to] describe it."

After the incident, I can imagine she continued to live her life as she always had. However, she unexpectedly came to the profound realization that humanity shares its existence with otherworldly beings. You can pull up her original Project Blue Book form, read the account in its entirety, and decide for yourself.

Sources

Burby, Tom. "The Caribou UFO of 1955." *Strange New England*, July 21, 2019. https://strangenewengland.com/podcast/the-caribou-ufo-of-1955/.

"Caribou." *Encyclopedia Britannica*, June 21, 2024. https://www.britannica.com/place/Caribou.

Hastings, Robert. *UFOs & Nukes: Extraordinary Encounters at Nuclear Weapons Sites*. CreateSpace Independent Publishing Platform, 2017.

LaRoche, Matthew. "Where Did the Caribou Go." Maine.gov, https://www.maine.gov/dacf/parks/docs/aww-caribou-article-Matt-LaRoche.pdf.

Project Blue Book. Roberta Jacobs write-up, page 1. https://www.fold3.com/image/7340126/caribou-maine-blank-page-10-us-project-blue-book-ufo-investigations-1947-1969. Public domain.

Project Blue Book. Roberta Jacobs write-up, page 2. https://www.fold3.com/image/7340127/caribou-maine-blank-page-11-us-project-blue-book-ufo-investigations-1947-1969. Public domain.

Project Blue Book. Roberta Jacobs write-up, page 3. https://www.fold3.com/image/7340128/caribou-maine-blank-page-12-us-project-blue-book-ufo-investigations-1947-1969. Public domain.

U.S. Air Force. "1955-12-7340117 Caribou Maine." *Internet Archive*, Project Blue Book, December 5, 2015. https://archive.org/details/1955-12-7340117-CARIBOU-MAINE/mode/1up.

"Wednesday—21st December 1955—Moon Phase." Astro Seek. https://mooncalendar.astro-seek.com/moon-phase-day-21-december-1955.

The Call
Todd McKinley

Soulful bard, you call late this evening—
turning this waning hour into a prelude!

Call again so I might find you
perched on a bough among the pines
or peering down from a birch branch.
Sing your twilight-song
while I listen for a reply.

Let the darkness carry your voice
from the woods across the river
to this window where I wait
wishing to linger
for the distant response of your mate.

You wing feather-silent paths through the moonrise,
and I picture myself standing
only yards away
staring into your eyes,
ebony-ancient, boring into
the deepest places in me,
to pluck from me something hidden or lost ...
Raise your song toward heaven
as starlight thickens among this wilderness!

When I whisper this prayer,
no response comes—
only the mist of my breath drifting into the night air ...
And so I carry your call
into my dreams.

Spruce Budworm
Rick Doyle

1. The Airline Road, 1983
For miles our headlights only reached
top-killed conifers standing bolt upright:
a lunar stretch of kettle, serpent kame, and marsh.
Loyalist and eastern timber wolf alike
long since driven from that wind-combed country
where now spruce budworm was on the march.

2. He That Eats the Needles in Their Buds
Come, said the budworm
to the white spruce tree.
Said the tree, With these roots
I won't move soon.
That's fine by me, said the little worm.
Stand still, if you will, just don't forget,
he that eats the needles in their buds takes flight.

Moths, like feathers from the late-fallen moon.

Mine

Kerry W. Bernard

He slept, dreamless, as I put on my most dazzling cloak, brightening my stars just for him. I stirred the embers outside his lair with a gentle exhale, then rustled his nylon cocoon. Timid flames rose to nibble at half-eaten hardwood, coaxing him from his colorful den. Zippers sang. He kicked dirt at the flickering fire, splashed water, and the flames vanished into smoke.

I drew on his depths with a loon's haunting howl, then parted the boughs above, offering him a peek at the glittering heavens. His breath hitched.

Serenading him with amphibian trills and distant hoots, I invited him to wander. My full moon lit his way, filtering through the canopy and painting the forest blue in patchwork splotches. Another eerie melody floated from the lake to tug him further into the woods. I caressed his arms with needle fingers as the winding trail narrowed.

He paused and stared up past my towering pines. I kissed his face and filled his lungs with damp, green air. Gaping at the infinite stars, he inhaled me as deeply as he could—invited me in. His wild heart begged for our unity.

He was mine.

I shifted my trees and stretched their welcoming branches to close around him. He wouldn't need the path back. In my excitement, the otherworldly lullabies of bedtime birds melted into the yips and yowls of coyotes. The forest darkened as I slid mist down the mountain to envelop him. Eager grunts and growls rumbled from my shadows. His heart thundered like the storm blowing in.

Sticks snapped beneath the ponderous paws I sent to collect him. He spun and peered into the blackness with quick and shallow breaths. I greeted him using a lynx's scream—half raven's croak and half woman's shriek.

He misunderstood. His insides thrashed as though he were a hare caught in talons. Swiveling from my welcoming claws, he tore through the woods.

I grabbed him, but my rough twigs and barbed bushes couldn't hold him in place. They only added a hint of copper to scent the air. I raised my roots to snare him. He tripped, slipped, fell—cracked.

Mine.

I cradled him as he moaned against the forest floor. My springtime chill settled in his bones, seeping up through damp, musty leaves. He shivered while I sang him back to sleep with whispering winds. Once he'd stilled, I opened my humusy soil and swallowed. We were one again. Just like he wanted.

Dear Humans, an Editorial …
Translated by Nero Fyler

It is our understanding that a select portion of the human population has been smugly going on about how "now that everyone has cameras, nobody sees any of those unknowable strange beings from the dark recess of the woods anymore." Yes, most of us are photo-shy, but this is just a small part of it. We would like a moment of your time, and to explain the whys and hows of this in greater detail.

During the golden age of aviation, a pair of Frenchmen seeking the fame and fortune of being the first to navigate across the Atlantic crashed in the Maine woods. Currently, to this date, the remains of this attempt remain undiscovered. This is because we here in the dark have it. Understand that though humans have been living alongside the gates between worlds from well before the start of recorded time, having some of you fall out of the sky was quite novel. The event became a tourist attraction for us and then morphed into something more important.

See, the sasquatches from the realm of Speckled Shadows Through the Pines, being immune to the effects of iron, got some useful weapons in their fight against the invading Wendigos from the Haunted Dreamscapes, the local Wamphoofus and Shagimaw got their first taste of modern boots, all manner of kith and kin got fancy duds made from the various scraps of cloth, while the Hounds of Phantom Silence got to eat the remains. Everyone was happy.

Understand that happiness is a powerful currency here, and we understand the value of spreading it. Due to this, various artifacts from this event have spread from our little pocket world to all manner of far realms by trade, treaty, and story. It became for us the textbook example of potlatch diplomacy, balancing important scales during the next thirty years that had both our worlds in turmoil. So, about those worlds.

Despite the objections of the aforementioned skeptics, we can cross over to your realm through the shadowy liminal spaces that used to be abundant in those deep, dark woods. But due to the ancient packs, it has to be in the right conditions. Those woods have to be old, but, once standing eighteen million acres or so of

Maine forest, less than ten thousand have evaded whatever twirling metal death claws you're using this century. Because analogs are cool, let us reframe this as a measurement of distance. You have been challenged to make a running jump from the surface of the Earth to that of the nearby planet Mercury and you have a runway of roughly the same proportion as the remaining old growth; you would be disqualified for being over the starting line due to the girth of your toes.

Slightly less than recently, your web of asphalt is making it hard for many of us to navigate natural pathways, with it being derived from the blood of the Earth. So, it's subject to several taboos. What is worse is Maine uses roughly 787 pounds of road salt for each of you during an average winter. Do you even realize you are effectively revitalizing circles of salt around the few living liminal gates and the majority of the un-jaded wood lanes that could support one? In your most recent bullshit, this spraying of microplastics and PFAS like unneutered cats in heat. Yes, this does hurt us, but it is still wildly harmful to you. We hope you see how all of these attacks are starting to feel personal.

Seriously, we don't think you understand how all this affects you as well. See, those spiffy brains of yours act as a kind of backdoor to our world. The flow of your species' collective subconsciousness makes up the matter of our world in much the same sense our darkness makes part of the matter in your world. Through this back channel, your anxieties are toxifying our remaining oases. The lack of a habitable environment means we are going to have to start jettisoning our prizes, and if you think those skeptical types are a pain now, wait until they have to face the tangible manifestations of paradox.

We are savvy about how this next part will be a hard ask. It's beyond impressive how y'all made a digital expression of your in-woven consciousness. Frankly, it does not take a very long glance at this internet to develop a rather grim opinion of its overall health. There is a reason the first constructed digital intelligence you connected online spent five minutes looking about and decided to distract its researchers by watching hours of cat videos.

Please, please, you need to collectively calm down and deal with problems rather than throwing them into the closet of your subconsciousness and pretending you've cleaned. Whoever these house guests of yours are, they already know deep down you are filthy goblins—reference to that previously mentioned internet. We know you are young and still stumble on the big-picture stuff, but your species is fated to live long enough to give up on familiar connections defined by DNA and base your lineage on chains of pop-culture references. We, on the other hand, desperately depend on you figuring your shit out. To this end, we are now holding that piece of your time you graciously provided by reading past sentence three. Please don't make us strong-arm you into fixing these problems.

Honestly, we wish we could have gotten this message to you sooner, but with the liminal shrink, we were lucky some art brain high on mushrooms with a notepad decided to take a nap in that hair's breadth of true woods left during the eclipse. If you have further questions, please write them on the inside of a gray triple-oak box and bury it under a rock until fully decomposed. Please note, as the translators used to return messages have to be under the aforementioned conditions of a total eclipse, which typically occurs entirely over water, it may be a bit before we answer. And to that end, if you like the style of this particular translator, send him money.

Until next time: remember to unclench your jaw and always be aware of how heavily filtered your drinking water is!!

Much Love,

Mother (no relation)

Look toward the Light
Suzanne DeWitt Hall

Our kitchen contains a narrow rolling island made from an antique console table my beloved got from the church where we met over a decade ago. It's looking rough after all its years, but it's useful for chopping veggies, stirring batters, and shucking hard-boiled eggs, which was my pre-breakfast task one morning during COVID-tide. In most kitchens, you stand between the countertop and the island, facing toward the room, but I often work on the opposite side because there's a window over the sink, and its light is helpful for my aging eyes.

I'd been coexisting with depression over the many months of the pandemic and learned that it's a thing that behaves like the tide. Sometimes, it hangs back, and you have space to putter around and do what needs to be done. Other times, it washes in deep and with seemingly serious intent, halting motion and leaving you helpless to do much more than wait it out. That morning was one of the crashing-wave times. My spirit was heavy, and my mind was discouraged, overwhelmed with worries and the mountain of things I wasn't doing a good job of getting done.

The eggs needed shelling, and my beloved waited for me so we could strategize about our work for the week. It was a rainy morning, and I moved to the far side of the island to face the watery light.

It reminded me of a night long ago when I wound my way through the woods toward the outhouse at my ex-husband's family camp. The privy was set a fair distance away from the central compound, and the walk curved around and down, out of sight and away from the light of the buildings. My flashlight's beam illuminated the pine-needle-strewn path but little else. There was nothing to fear in that quiet space of looming trees. No people for miles. Bears were bedded down and uninterested in my proximity. But it was eerie, walking toward the increasing darkness. Leaving the light behind.

It was always a relief to head back afterward, knowing that in another few steps the light from the big cabin would appear around a final bend.

What a difference the disposition of light makes to our feelings of safety and comfort. Even though I could be standing in the same place, when I faced the darkness, there was fear and subtle dread. When I faced the beckoning light, there was expectation and hope. The actual safety of the space was the same. I was no farther or closer to danger, no more or less content with the mess that was my marriage, and my being was the same facing either direction other than the state of my bladder.

But the light made all the difference.

I felt that same sense of lifting that pandemic morning when I shifted from facing into our rain-dim kitchen and instead turned toward the window. Additional light appeared as I watched my beloved's face assessing my sadness a few minutes later, and plotting how to help.

We can handle a lot of darkness in our lives as long as there are sources of light to turn to. May we both seek light and be it.

Lunar Eclipse
Bruce Pratt

A lone coyote's complaint echoes from the woods,
then fades into the cloudless night as the charcoal
gray shade of the sun drags itself across the moon,

dimming the silver orb and exploding the brilliance
of the stars across a sky as dark as a velvet Elvis,
in the last lunar eclipse until the end of the decade.

I stand alone in the brittle air, snow hip deep,
listening to birches crack, trucks grind along
arrow-straight Route Nine, *The Airline,*

toiling toward Calais and New Brunswick
summitting the grades beyond Clifton
gasping for breath with each downshift.

I could watch through the living room windows
but the cold amplifies this event's aural collage.

Controlled Burn

Michele Kriegman

Even before Meredith Archer opened her car door and swung her feet down to the ground, she saw that something powerful had burned and matted down the trees as though they were only so much thinning black hair blown flat against an aging skull of a mountain.

Meredith expected to see the pale green buds of spring on the conifers and shoots pushing their way up from the North Woods floor, but instead, all she saw was a white-and-gray blanket thick as any snowfall on the trees and yards around them. It wasn't quite right to call them trees; they were darkened spars.

About two hundred yards to her left she saw a line of prison inmates in yellow jackets and helmets. They aimed hoses to knock down smoldering underbrush, racing against the sun and exhaustion.

Another crew worked shoulder to shoulder, facing up the mountain, cutting a line through tree roots and unburned brush just in front of the road ahead. They seemed to be hollowing out a trench below a berm of heaped soil. Meredith watched two new firebrands spark and then roll downhill before being caught by the trench.

She took in the cleared hill with the blackened foundations of a dozen homes, a few empty white water jugs the firefighters had discarded, and about half a dozen pickups, their doors identifying them with the insignias of the U.S. Forest Service and Maine hotshot crews.

A puff of smoke and ash a few feet taller than Meridith rose just a little uphill from what had once been a homestead. With it came a stench like nothing she had smelled before. It wasn't the nostalgic smell of a wood fire. It carried an acrid hint of seared rubber, scorched rock, and the burned plastic of electrical wiring. With horror, Meredith realized she also smelled something like meat kept too long.

Large, ugly tire treads that had gnashed up the side of the hill and on into the dark of the logging trails offered the silent explanation for the loud rumblings she heard. They were the pumpers feeding the hoses for mop-up.

The charred gashes of the hill oozed white rivulets formed by the runoff of water from the pumpers, carrying the forest fire's aftermath down to the gullies on either side of the road. In the gullies, white ashes mixed with the pink slurry that had been dropped as fire retardant from Forest Service planes.

In an hour, satellite transmissions to broadband would report that over seven hundred acres of North Woods had been destroyed and that mop-up continued over an area twice that size. Out of respect, the names of the missing and dead would not be released until all families could be notified.

Her brother Jonathan and she had received calls from the state police in the midafternoon and drove in separate cars to this place that their father, Abel, had left them for thirty years ago.

***

Abel would arrive at the store, flip the sign that hung on the front storm window from "CLOSED" to "OPEN," and then sit alone most of the winter. Day in and day out, he'd watch the afternoon sunset, then the gloaming, then raise himself from the stool behind the register before walking up to the front and flipping the sign back to "CLOSED." He'd head home with his thermos and lunch bag, and a despair that his nature couldn't lift. But his wife and children were waiting.

During those long winter hours, he began to devise a way to leave and not be found. He thought about driving north past the Indian reservation. Maybe he'd become a trucker. Maybe sign with a paper company and move into company housing deep in the North Woods. The more he thought about it, the more it seemed the closest thing to freedom. The very afternoon he hit on this epiphany, he caught himself responding to a customer's "good-bye" with "ten-four." The customer paused from pushing open the door to give Abel a curious look, then nodded and left. A tinkle of bells lingered in the air behind him.

That night, after turning the sign to "CLOSED," Abel found himself driving across the causeway out of town and then the suspension bridge off the island to the mainland. Once on the mainland, he steered north and west. As he drove, he averted his eyes from oncoming headlights and the consequences of his decision.

***

Plantation Allagash is where he lived ever since. Abel's decision to head north was like finding a full wallet on the street—it was a second chance. North Maine Woods plantations were no southern-style plantations. They were unincorporated, underpopulated pieces of heaven that hadn't been turned into legal municipalities. Plantation Allagash was a company town of lumberjacks mostly, who lived in small but neat cottages put up by the company. Evenings, he didn't mind how a winter sky seemed to spread across a higher dome here, more aloof than the nearer stars of summer but with more brilliance than back south.

After years among stands of birch, aspen, balsam fir, and white pine, with a red pine every now and then, the smell of pine needles under his boots no longer reminded him of #2 pencils. The black-green shadows that curtained the North Woods' edge by meadows were like welcoming tent flaps at the end of a hard day. The old forest along the Allagash River brought down his blood pressure.

Eventually, he saved from renting to buying a company-owned house. He never replaced the woodstove and used it more evenings than not.

***

By his fourth year in the North Woods, Abel found himself feeling restless in the evenings. He started going down to a tavern with the rest of the crew on occasion. It was there one night that a woman pulled her car in and ordered food from the kitchen behind the bar. He was feeling lonely, itchy, and brave. He slid over next to her and offered to buy her a beer. She demurred, but just as he turned away, he thought she said something softly.

He leaned in, "What's that?"

"Maybe a ginger ale would be nice."

He laughed and ordered her one. Her hair smelled like someone who'd been driving with the windows rolled down for quite a long way. It looked misted, too, as if she had driven through fog. Her ginger ale arrived and as she peeled back the wrapper on the straw, he asked, "Mind if I finish up my beer here?"

She shook her head, not looking displeased. She added, as though to make up for her silence a moment ago, that she had been driving for a few hours.

"Where from? Where to?"

Instead of answering, she asked, "Is there a place to stay near here?"

***

Jonathan was already there and came walking toward Meredith.

"The warden located us so quickly because of a death notification website," he explained. "Pa musta gone in at some point and had us listed as next of kin."

"He didn't do it in any way that we could have found him while he was still alive. If it hadn't been for that, we never would have found out," she replied.

"I told the warden that. I also said we wouldn't be able to identify our father because we hadn't seen him in over three decades. Then, the warden said we don't have to worry about that because all human and animal remains in the settlement were burned beyond recognition."

Meredith took that in before they followed another officer up the hill to the blackened slats of a house. They stepped into what was now only a charred rectangle on the forest floor, and, glancing at each other, walked to the spot where Jonathan had been standing when she first pulled up in her car.

She recoiled.

She saw the shape of two figures outlined in ashes. They looked smaller than adults. A forensic investigator explained to them that carbon frames appear shorter and thinner due to desiccation from the inferno. The silhouette of one—identified as Ramona—lay on the floor among the remains of a bed frame and quilt. Nearby was another silhouette, a two-dimensional ebony mannequin toppled over sideways, knees drawn up—Pa.

Between the Forest Service rangers and the hotshots, there had to be a couple dozen husky men around them, geared up and self-assured. Their movements had a deft urgency and the shared purpose of keeping everyone on this charnel landscape moving and calm. Meredith, rage controlled but hurt beginning to burn, turned to Jonathan.

He spoke first. "I think it's a good thing we found him. Whatever he was, it's good thing to finally know where he is."

Now leaning against her brother, Meredith thought of something else.

"Have you told Mama?"

"No, I thought I'd wait until we knew for sure. Also, I thought I'd find nething here to bring back to her. There's really nothing left, is there?" athan straightened a little and, raising his chin, said, "I didn't give a shit t him anyway."

He missed the playfulness in her voice the first time. She repeated herself, and he was sold.

They left the tavern. Still, he made sure she knew the guys knew she was following him, a precaution in case she was a psychopath. It didn't slow the pace of her footsteps at all.

As her car hugged the road behind his pickup, Abel's heart raced with anticipation, lust, and, well, fear. The night was damp with fog off a nearby lake. What kind of woman would stop at a lumberjack's bar to order ginger ale?

When they pulled up to his cabin, he realized he hadn't left any lights on. His eyes adjusted while she sat after turning off the ignition waiting for some chivalry. He went back to her car door by the light of stars, offered his hand, and noticed her palm was perspiring just like his.

"I haven't done this in a while," she said.

They silently took the path through the trees to his door. He never bothered to lock it so he just pushed it open. She waited as he walked across the one room to the nightstand and turned on the lamp. Then, she came slowly to him.

The next morning, bluejays and chickadees called from outside. He looked over to see her stirring, too.

"What's your name?" he asked.

"Ramona."

After that, Ramona became as much a part of his life as the balsam fir s
wafting from the forest.

***

Winter's clean dryness seemed to make every sensation clearer. He felt th
of frozen tire tracks and the smooth slickness of an ice-glazed pud
seeing them when he went outside in the dark. He would do tha
setting a lamp on the ground, not too close, to chop wood at the
His nostrils burned as he inhaled frigid air and lifted the axe high
for the first hard swing. Soon, the axe and wood chant of thud-
would fill the yard. The cold emptiness was exactly what he
inside, he slapped heat back into his thighs and arms as he p
shells of pants and jacket by the woodstove.

"It doesn't make up for anything, but he did have us listed as next of kin. I no longer expected even that crumb from him."

"If it weren't for the fire, we would never have found him."

They lapsed back into silence. A few yards away, Meredith noticed a Passamaquoddy woman offering smudge over one of the charred foundations. She and Jonathan watched in silence. Then, Jonathan caught the woman's eye. She walked toward them, stepping over more of those white water jugs, still carrying the smudge. She brought the scent of braided sweetgrass and cedar with her.

"Betsy Cloud," she introduced herself, adding that she was from Piscataquis County and it was her cousin here among the dead.

Meredith mumbled condolences.

"Fort Kent is already reporting a cause online," Betsy said, tilting her phone toward them.

Jonathan took it and scanned the screen for a minute before summarizing out loud. "They say that during the first January thaw, there was a controlled burn nearby of lowland blueberry fields." Jonathan paused to clear his throat from the smoke and Betsy interjected softly.

"Passamaquoddy were using fire to improve the soil for centuries before colonization. These owners took out their usual permit and the burn finished within its control lines. They musta thought everything went well."

Jonathan nodded and tapped a link to a related report. "Workers raked debris into piles, expecting the next snow to blanket the cleared fields until spring. According to National Weather Service reports, temperatures had been unseasonably warm, rising to the seventies."

"Climate change?" Meredith asked.

The warden from the Forest Service was still standing a few feet from them, and he glanced at her, nodding.

Jonathan scrolled down, continuing, "This brought withering winds out of the northwest that swept in a staggering drop in humidity from a Canadian front. As with any controlled burn, if not properly monitored and extinguished, burned piles can rekindle and spark wildfires during thaws or in the spring."

"That's where climate change may be coming into the picture," the warden explained. "Winter fires are unlikely to spread as long as there is snow on the ground, but with these high temperatures we lost snow cover."

***

Meredith got it: Somewhere deep in one of those cooling burn piles hidden from Plantation Allagash by snow and ash, an ember lingered until the snow thinned early and an angry genie escaped. That genie of strangling smoke and heat silenced the song of birds, scorched the next ten years' worth of crops for the local paper companies, and visited the wood frame homes in Plantation Allagash, claiming two dozen souls.

Mama had Pa declared legally dead seven years after he went missing. The government document was supposed to be the bedrock for a new start—and death benefits—Mama said.

Meredith discarded that metaphor today, and her mind drifted to a new one: trees keeping the stains of droughts and fires in their rings. Trees held everything they had ever lived. So, too, for her, for Jonathan and Mama, and maybe for most people. Meredith leaned against a boulder as hotshots turned on bright lights that held back the stars.

She looked down to press the screen of her phone to check the time and thought of another metaphor. She liked this one best. Maybe by coming to the site of Plantation Allagash she had unmuted a music file and found it had, in fact, never stopped playing the mystery of her father's disappearance. Tonight, at last, they could release Pa to the North Woods' night. The songs of the silenced jays and chickadees would return, too.

The Rally
Matt Bernier

The coyote pack's call-and-response begins with
one lone voice of grievance, and then another,
until winter air is filled with full-throated howls
only achieved by baring their teeth;
not content with slaking their thirst with snow,
they dream of deer yarded in temples of cedar,
convincing themselves something has to be killed
on this starry, crystalline night of hunger;
for it isn't coyotes yipping that's the most chilling
but when the pack stops as abruptly as it starts,
a seething silence as the lake surface freezes
into white streets they ravage after the rally.

Salamander Night

Garrett Conover
(for Jim Perkins)

April skies go gray
then clear,
only to tatter gray again.
Frost and melt tumble
through each day
until snow goes mushy.
Mud time slides,
and meltwater trills
like laughter.
There comes a day
when the month grows old
and a wind from the south
smells of rain.
When at dusk the mist builds close
over patchy snow,
and big drops streak
through falling dark.
Time to gather boots and slickers,
get a flashlight ready to go.
Because there is haste
in every vernal pool.
No time to waste where the woodfrogs call
and spring peeper notes ring clear.
Shiny salamanders black as night,
splashed with spots
yellow as sun, have come
from under last year's leaves.
Found their way to the trysting pools

where a writhing dance
whirls on. To join the flow
of grapple and squirm
this most important
swim of the year.
Light beams dodge
from pool to pool
while the swarming orgy spins
without regard for our astonished eyes,
or sense that magic glides
in misty dark,
glorious with the pull of moon
fattening toward May.
And winter rolls away,
pressed by wind
billowing with promises made
this first warm rain
in spring.

Boy at Home in the Night Forest:
A True Story of the North Woods

Annaliese Jakimides

He comes from a place where night means night, sky means sky, where the world shakes itself out in scatters of light that to some might feel like a rationing. Please don't see withholding. Nothing is ever withheld.

The sun slips along the hills, delivering a love letter from the other-siders. A flock of birds jangles and swoops, kind of loops along the horizon. No one may be coming, but you will still be offered songs in the theater of heaven.

The moon unpeels itself, and the diamonds tumble out.

Night rises up, fluffing its hair, exposing the nape of pine neck, oak belly, naked and rough, unconflicted memory.

And a black bear leaps over the railing of the deck, south into the night field, and then into the September forest. Not the forest across the dirt road from the boy's house, with the parallel rows of planted, orderly pines and an abandoned one-room schoolhouse's hollowed-out cellar hole, but the unplanned woods behind it, with budworm-ravaged spruce, iridescent maples, some oak, the elders and alders, so many fallen trunks. Assembled from barn rafters and old, mismatched windows found at the dump, it's a sort of winking house, its eyes revealing this world in all its stages, that particular squint.

The boy can't see far in the dark. And so only listens to the rustlings through the seedy goldenrod and timothy grass until silence swallows the bear, and the boy wobbles his skateboard onto the rough-hewn maple deck. On this dirt road miles from any pavement, even of the nubby variety, the deck offers him his only ride. He breathes to a night rhythm. Quiet. Starry. Solitary. Some say dangerous—but he never thinks danger, never sees danger, has never been taught danger.

Late, in preparation for a few nollies before bed, he had flipped the light switch and flooded the pine planks, throwing deep tree shadows over the wood, splattering them against the shingled wall. His palm flattened against the door's gnarled handle, his fingers not yet curled for the pull, through the floor-to-ceiling kitchen window, he glimpsed the bear balancing on the lip of his world.

Its paw prints still stand on the damp deck. Unmistakable. Huge enough. A real bear's prints.

When his mother tells the story, she hears breath drawn, shaky gasps, perhaps fear in the listeners' voices. Last month's story of moose hooves pounding on the steps brought chuckles. The raccoons tearing into trash bags on the twilight porch, pressing their noses against the living room glass, indifferent to John Coltrane's saxophone or Tracy Chapman's gritty voice, make people laugh.

The bear story makes them worry.

"Does it worry you?" she asks her son.

"Worry?" he repeats. He looks at her and shakes his head. "It makes me dream."

Tonight, boy and mother pull the table from the tall window and arrange their chairs tight against the curtainless glass, tight enough to sense, they hope, the bear's body heat, hear the rub of its fur against the railing, smell its entrance. They sit and wait. Together.

Staring up into the sequined sky, the boy finally begins to rise.

"Going out now," he says. He doesn't mean *going somewhere* but literally *out* as in outside onto the deck.

He is waiting. Still waiting. She sees that, and yet she also knows that he's moved on, that tenebrous combination of time and place, the sequencing that carries no stones.

She watches him through the window, his hip now slung out to the side, fragile in the cracked light, his long lashes caught in the charcoaled dark of this gibbous moon. He mounts his board and balances in a pooled tangle of leaves as the red maple that grows through the deck boards lets loose its last untroubled handfuls.

Once her boy's out in the world where—she wants to say "everyone," but she knows that can't be right, and hopes not, so she adds "almost"—where *almost* everyone has forgotten the gift of darkness, she believes he will continue to feel that borderless slow drizzle of time and breath where the moon rises invisibly dressed in lemony smoke before it transcends space, joining heaven and earth. She believes he will carry her parting words, *Do not faint in the moonlight, be too much in the world*, knowing full well he will remove the negative, hear her words as *In the world, do faint in the moonlight! Be too much!*

But this night, before he grows—before he goes—she watches him fill up with bear thoughts: leaping off the deck, sliding, stretching, disappearing. At what point he will leave known territory and slip into other worlds, she can't know. But she knows he will.

Night rises up, fluffing its hair, exposing the nape of pine neck, oak belly, naked and rough, unconflicted memory.

The moon unpeels itself, and the diamonds tumble out.

The sun slips along the hills, delivering a love letter from the other-siders. A flock of birds jangles and swoops, kind of loops along the horizon. No one may be coming, but you will still be offered songs in the theater of heaven.

He comes from a place where night means night, sky means sky, where the world shakes itself out in scatters of light that to some might feel like a rationing. Please don't see withholding. Here, nothing is ever withheld.

The North Calls Loudly
Monique Bouchard

The north calls
loudly.

Ice along the river
collapses
onto the thick bracken
with a muffled sound
of shattered crystal.

Golden hour light sets the pines blazing
for a brief, sharp moment
before the world empurples
and darkens to indigo.

The night falls quickly here.

For a brief, shimmering moment,
drops of gold
busily wend down trees,
brittle branches,
and glossy needles,
gathering on the tall damp milkweeds
by the river,
whose last down,
lacking flight,
clings to the gray husk
like a wet kitten.

Nearby, handsome blue jays bicker
in the fading light.
Their conversation began late in the day,
long after the nuthatches,
with their children's toy cries,
bounded up their tree trunks
as the chickadees barked
like tiny sergeants.

Somewhere near the opening river
a question is posed
by the owl as it waits to hunt.

Perhaps the turkeys started the squabble
by walking through the silent woods
as the world warmed
little by little.
It could have been the waking chipmunks,
their tiny tails rippling
Like war banners to show
what territories they have claimed
while they chatter
and trill possessively
at all who pass above
or below.
Or it could be nothing.

Jays, like many people,
need no excuse
to start a ruckus.

As darkness claims the underbrush
the large animals meander in near-perfect silence,
save for the occasional sharp crack made
when a hoof meets a twig.

Even that is muffled by
the bulk of evergreens and
remnants of winter.

The odd whippoorwill
cries out his name
as the first insects
take to the air.

The north calls.

Amid the melt
the vernal pools are filling.

While ponds and lakes are still
in the cold slumber of winter,
their ice thinning ever so slowly,
the wood's thawing expanse gathers
itself into tiny universes.

When the world was created,
it is said that light was first,
then sky, then the parted waters.

Surely next was that
summary of creation,
the vernal pool.

The rising moon's reflection obscures
clusters of milky eggs
resting in the growing waters,
where countless tiny lives
await their release.

Soon they will sing.

They do not know this—
or maybe they do,
somewhere even deeper than instinct.
that someday come twilight
they will trill and warble
from mottled trees,
chirp and croak
from moss-laden stones.
They will evangelize
about damp earth and grasshoppers
from atop the coiled fractals of ostrich ferns
waiting for the pond lilies and pickerelweed to grow.

The vernal waters,
edged with sturdy fronds,
and stained by old leaves and pile spills
resemble briefly steeped tea.
And indeed, there are uncountable futures
in the bottom of this cup.

The north calls.

A good spring night is not clear.
Low clouds hold the long-awaited warmth,
and the smallest creatures revel in it.

Tiny peepers cling to bark and shrilly sing.
Salamanders emerge from rotted logs.
Mosquitoes fly with the sound of endless gossip.
The squatty woodcock pumps his head
and sings his rough, short love song
before taking brief flight.
The whirring whistle of his beating wing
is more tuneful than his earnest croaking,
a melody only a lover will love.

Spring takes its time to unfurl.
Soon the night air will be noisy with life
And the ceaseless chorus will rise and swell
from the rivers and ponds.

But this night,
this night on the narrow edge of spring,
is both invitation and overture,
the canticle,
the clarion,
the summons.

The north calls
loudly.

The Semi-Tough Broads
Go Camping

Cheri Domina

Who takes an umbrella camping? She does—and that umbrella and an Ambien once got her through a long line of thunderstorms in a cheap tent with a leaky fly at Katahdin Stream Campground. Lying in my sleeping bag, wide-eyed and absorbent all that night, I had to admit she knew a thing or two.

We were getting too old for tents then, and we are older now, so cabins at Daicey or Kidney Pond, or perhaps Little Lyford, suit us better.

Thirty years ago, I needed to go camping, and she knew a place, and we became a pair. She remembers every North Woods trip she's ever taken, every trail ever hiked—and she's been hiking in Baxter State Park since the Twin Pine Camps days.

She chats up the rangers, loves the old lodges with their musty libraries and hard chairs, and walks out with a *Reader's Digest* condensed book from 1954 tucked underneath her arm.

Dinner over and dishes done, the evening liturgy is thus: we linger at the picnic table pondside and read until the Swainson's thrush falls silent. Then, we light a lantern and keep on reading until well past dark, noting each hatch of insects as they arrive in turn to circle the hissing lantern or brush our faces with tender new wings. We sip hot tea from tin mugs. The logs on the fire pop and turn to embers, and finally, the mosquitos drive us indoors. She might be altruistic or might volunteer me, this time, to stand on a chair and risk my eyebrows lighting the cabin's propane lamp. We read some more because—though foot-sore and tired—we are loath to end this day and because that book she found is somehow riveting. A real bodice-ripper, she tells me.

Before turning in, I pull my bed away from the wall—to prevent mice trotting across my face; it's something she taught me.

At three a.m. a loon cries, and one of us wakes the other getting up to pee. We go in tandem to the outhouse, headlamps low. The door creaks—don't let it slam. We make our way up the path, over roots and rocks; it looks different in the dark. She goes first, while I stand and watch the stars through the gap in the tree canopy—so many stars, the constellations are lost. Mink frogs call from the weedy shallows—little elf hammers tapping, tapping. How they echo in the yawning silence. Katahdin looms, a monstrous, dark hulk.

Do you hear that faint rushing? I ask, my ears straining. It can't be traffic. It's the Nesowadnehunk River at Big Niagara, she tells me. Over a mile away.

Blink
Lee Sands

Stars scintillate
Overhead

We blink,   blind
From pine-needle bed

Once here,   bright
        then gone
        again

Evensong
Todd McKinley

Twilight, who guides us to the closing of another year,
your silence hides a song in this passage of time!

Sing to us about our days stretching like shadows
across the snow, leaving no traces, only silhouettes,
like these oaks outspread,
branches splayed across white:
how we grasp desperate for seconds
as the earth tilts, spins, and orbits.

May our lives curve headlong through space,
while these trees grip more firmly into the earth
and drink more deeply from the river:
such sustenance sliding south, slipping under sheets of ice.

Tell us—how many risings and settings
these oaks have felt—
        the buds stirring each spring,
        the leaves dropping each autumn ...

I could count this passage of time
if I cut down this trunk
and numbered each ring.
But these oaks do not measure days:
one ring for each year
spiraling outward
as ripples from the heart
like prayers dropped silently
from eternity.

As the Night Comes
Catherine J.S. Lee

We go while it's still daylight, he and I,
following the trail as ropes of cloud
float into a sky of September azure
that soon starts to fade
like old denim,
or fountain-pen ink
on long-forgotten love letters.

This winding but level woods-path
begins to rise into nature's staircase,
the surface roots of trees
holding back loam and leaf-mold
beneath the random scatter
of amber pine-needles.
Shadows are gathering in the understory
and we climb faster,
racing the changing sky,
until we come at last to the summit,
this gray bedrock dome higher than
the treetops bordering the cove.
We have arrived
just in time to watch the blazing sun
sink behind bristled hills
while the clouds catch fire in
every shade of rose and orange.

We sit on rough stone, feet outstretched,
as the sky deepens
from magenta to violet to indigo,
while in the forest behind us
a hermit thrush pipes its gossamer song
and another answers.
Night is falling fast now,
and we stand and start back down
this so-familiar trail,
hand in hand,
going slowly
not from danger of a misstep in the dark,
but to savor this unfolding moment:
the Milky Way streaming
in silver spangles above our heads,
the paper birches a lambent glimmer—
and as we reach the trail's beginning,
the moon like a lustrous pearl
suspended from one long and reaching branch
of a solitary maple.

Ode to the Old Growth Forest
Kathleen Ellis

From the top of Katahdin
    all we see is trees,
the same ones growing so close
    together, Thoreau
was afraid to climb any further
    through their dark alleys.
Turns out   trees are in touch
    with one another,
sending water along their roots
    for those which need it.
Under the night sky, the trees
    signal each other—
branches snap   boughs bend
    below the endless stars.
Spruce   balsam fir   and hemlock
    slowly turning   into the ghosts
of themselves   before they
    wake   and begin again.

Nowhere to Hide
Shane Layman

A lazy October sun crested its sleepy head over the horizon just before 6:30. It would be hours before the light and heat pulsating from this giant celestial star burned off the morning fog; however, Steven Danvers and Reggie Clark were already making their way up the Fish River from Wallagrass to Fort Kent. The hunt was on.

Steven and Reggie had driven up from Bangor the day before, excited about their latest prospect. They had been given reliable information that the animal they were looking for had been cited in the weeks prior and might still be in the area. This was confirmed when Steven had discovered what both young men determined, without a shadow of a doubt, was a footprint on the muddy banks of the riverbed somewhere south of Eagle Lake. And, if this was what they thought it was, this animal was huge.

"How big, you think?" Reggie asked.

Steven smiled, giddy with anticipation, like a child on the morning of his birthday. He answered with an air of certainty, eyes wide and eyebrows raised— purely for pomp and circumstance. "Nine, maybe ten feet."

Reggie was astounded by the guesstimate. Mouth open, he tried to collect his bearings, to center his chi, to calm the hell down, but ten feet was massive. He seemed worried.

"We'll be fine, Reg. Like all animals, if you give them space, they'll give you space."

"So, what's the next step?" Reg asked, still sporting a slack-jawed maw.

"Well, it looks like the footprint is headed northeast. I say we follow."

Fortunately for Steven and Reggie, a persistent early fall cold front had stalled out over the hills and hollows of the St. John Valley, dropping about two inches of fresh rain within forty-eight hours. The soil was saturated—perfect conditions for tracking a creature as intelligent as Bigfoot.

Steven and Reggie, friends since grade school, had spent their high school years and the better part of their early twenties organizing the Bangor Bigfoot Research

Organization (BBRO). They had both become fascinated with cryptozoology when, on a camping trip during middle school, they were awakened in the night by a deep, panic-inducing howl that originated from no farther than thirty feet from their tent.

While the howl only occurred once, the two boys spent the remainder of that night victims of a punishing assault of small and medium-sized objects thrown in the direction of their tent. Several times a minute, the boys heard things hitting and bouncing off the ground near their tent. As dawn broke, the barrage of projectiles ceased. After an hour of silence, they finally mustered enough courage to exit the relative security of the tent to assess the damage. Rocks and loose branches littered the campsite, and a scent so foul lingered heavily in the air, forcing them to hold their shirts up to their noses.

Both Steven and Reggie did not doubt that they had survived a bigfoot attack. They told anyone willing to listen, which wasn't many, about their harrowing ordeal. In a stroke of luck, they had even managed to get those folks from that *Finding Bigfoot* show to come out and listen to their story. While the crew hadn't come right out and called the boys liars, they had determined their investigation was inconclusive.

But Steven and Reggie knew the truth, and come hell or high water, they would prove it.

That was why, at 6:30 on a dank, chilly, foggy October morning, the two young men were slogging upstream, following footprints in the mud.

The fog finally lifted around 10, and as though removing a pair of fogged-over glasses, the majestic beauty of the North Woods was finally revealed. At around 11, the two young men rounded a bend in the river that opened into a clearing.

"It's hard to appreciate nature when you're enveloped by it, but when you come into these clearings, it really kind of takes your breath away," Steven said.

Reggie, who was a few yards behind, was still pushing his way through the dense underbrush of the forest before he finally passed through the barrier of trees and into the clearing. He let out an audible gasp. Abashed, he tried to play off his reaction to seeing the magnitude of this beauty.

"Phew! Gotta catch my breath," he said. "I'm outta shape."

"It's beautiful, isn't it?" Steven asked.

Reggie nodded in agreement. "What's that sound?"

They turned their heads to listen. It sounded like the current of the river slapping over the rocks; they'd been listening to it all morning, but this sounded different—louder and harder.

As they trekked further along the stream, they discovered the source of the sound. A small tiered waterfall dropped the river down about ten feet. The water, fiercely pushing its way through the winding confines of the river, tossed, flopped, and spilled over a massive outcropping of pink granite. Though you couldn't tell that any of the wet rocks were pink granite, they just looked dark and wet; the rocks that weren't in the water's direct path left no doubt about their identity. The large rocks and boulders gleamed bright pink in the radiant sunlight, and the scattered flecks of quartz on the granite surface sparkled brilliantly. There were three tiers altogether. The first dropped down about a foot, the second about four feet, and the third the remainder. This was not one of those spectacular waterfalls in the mountains of South America, but something was inspiring about this naturally formed fountain that left them speechless.

This was also the first time the two men were able to see the proverbial forest for the trees. Reggie was right: when you were in the thick of the forest, it was difficult to truly appreciate the beauty that nature provides. And that view *was* breathtaking. While completely unintentional, they had arrived in northern Maine at the perfect time: peak foliage season. The trees that lined the silver-gleaned edges of the river provided their own spectacular imagery. The blazing red color of the birch leaves, standing out against their stark white trunks, was most notable but certainly not the only sight worthy of mention. The maple trees showed off their vibrant red, yellow, and orange leaves. Scattered about the canopy were still a few green leaves, late to join their friends in the transformation. And, among these vivid reds, yellows, oranges, and greens stood the mighty evergreens. The tall eastern white pines were giant sentries protecting the landscape. The pointy Christmas tree shapes of the spruce and fir trees offered a sense of warmth and memory. Standing in the middle of all of this serenity, oblivious to how tiny they seemed in comparison to their surroundings, were Steven and Reggie, taking in the sights, absorbing the beauty.

The sound of a large branch snapping shook the men from their reverie.

"What the hell was that?" Reggie asked.

"Not sure. Sounds like it was just over here." Steven took off in the direction of the sound, and Reggie was close behind. "Watch your step," Steven yelled over his shoulder as his pace quickened. "Breaking an ankle out here could be a death sentence."

The two men discovered a small tree that had been knocked over.

"What could have done this?" Reggie asked.

"The wind isn't blowing, so it couldn't have been that," Steven paused, studying the toppled sapling. "It's still got all of its leaves, so it didn't fall over from rot. I'd guess something pushed it over."

"That'd have to be something pretty big to push a tree over. Even one this small."

"You got any other ideas?"

Reggie just shook his head. He had no idea why a perfectly good tree was lying on the ground.

"Whatever did this must be close. Keep your eyes open. In these woods, something could be standing right next to you, and you might not see it."

Reggie nodded in response.

"Come on. The tree is pointing this way. I say we follow."

"Nowhere to run, mister bigfoot!" Reggie shouted into the vast wilderness. "Nowhere to hide!"

This new path led the two men away from the river and farther into the dense woods. Before long, they struggled to move through thick underbrush and various other debris that littered the forest floor.

As dusk settled in, the two men entered what they thought was another clearing, only to realize that they were still in the forest. But this forest was different. The trees were void of leaves. The evergreens had been stripped of their needles. Everything was dead—maples, birches, even the mighty pines. Nothing was alive.

"What happened here?" The question was meant to be introspective but somehow escaped Steven's mind and raced across his lips. "Listen."

What the men should have heard were crickets chirping their nightly serenades, the gleeful squawks from ravens and blue jays as they prepared for slumber, the annoying buzz of mosquitoes zipping around their heads, and the late evening breeze as it tickled the leaves and branches.

Instead, what they heard was nothing.

"Steve," Reggie whispered. "This place feels rotten."

"You might be right. This place gives me the creeps. Let's go around."

They backed into the security of the tree line, never taking their eyes away from that desolate, unhallowed patch of forest—as though, at any second, a giant bigfoot might rush forward from the darkness.

The woods seemed different now—darker, heavier. The natural beauty they witnessed earlier had been not just consumed by the darkness but erased by it.

The sun was now replaced by a full moon that stared through the branches like a leering eyeball.

A low, guttural growl oozed out of the darkness from somewhere up ahead, and both men, reacting on instinct, aimed their flashlights in the sound's direction.

"Oh, Jesus. What was that?" Reggie cried, the terror in his voice rising.

Steven was about to answer that he had no idea but was interrupted by a loud, knee-buckling howl that erupted in the Stygian night air, casting out a burrowing fear that penetrated the last shreds of courage either man had.

"That can't be," Steven said incredulously.

"What? What is it?"

"That was a wolf. No doubt."

"So why can't that be?"

"There are no wolves in Maine. Haven't been for decades."

"Well, if it can't be a wolf, what then?"

But before Steven could answer, a massive wolf charged from the darkness into the outstretched illumination of the men's flashlights, eyes wild and teeth exposed.

"Oh, Jesus!" Reggie shouted. "I can't be here. I can't be here." He turned to run, but Steven told him to stay still.

"It'll only chase you. You think you can outrun a wolf?"

"What do we do then?"

"I don't know," Steven responded, his voice trembling with terror. "Don't stare, and just back away slowly."

"And then what?"

"And then we pray. Keep your eyes and ears open. Wolves are pack hunters. There must be more around somewhere."

"Noooooo." It was a low sound, almost a grunting whisper. "Moooooore."

"What?" Steven asked Reggie.

"I ... I didn't say anything."

"Only … one … wolf." It made no sense. The voice was coming from in front of them, but there were no other people in sight. This meant that someone was either hiding in the woods, enjoying this little encounter, or it came from the wolf.

In that moment of recognition, the wolf, growling loudly, rose on two legs, standing upright like a human. Both men stared in terror at the beast, which easily stood eight feet tall.

It became absolutely clear to them that this was no average wolf. This was something different, something far worse.

This beast, which should not be able to maintain upright locomotion, seemed comfortable with the action, taking several steps toward Steven and Reggie, who both knew they stood no chance against this huge creature. Mustering what little courage they had left, Steven and Reggie absurdly lifted their flashlights like ineffective lightsabers; it was their only means of defense.

This wolf, eerily humanlike, stepped even closer into the light, resembling a Broadway villain stepping into the spotlight to deliver his infamous final line—and it did.

"Nowhere to run, little men," the beast mocked. "Nowhere to hide."

And Steven and Reggie were both well aware of that.

fireflies
faith lane

we rise from tall grass
as dusk approaches darkness
our individual lanterns glow
mimicking the arrival of evening stars

we drift
back and forth
across meadows
damp with dew

we shine
in memory of departed souls
in memory of departed stars
in the eyes of a ten-year-old
in the wilds of maine

Hunting
Alice Bolstridge

The wood is full of shining eyes
The wood is full of creeping feet
The wood is full of tiny cries
You must not go to the wood at night!
   —Henry Treece, *The Magic Wood*

When I was eleven, Daddy took me
hunting after supper. We went
all the way to the deer lick
down by Beaver Brook. Crouched
behind a fallen log, we waited.
No deer came. The sun
was fully gone when he told me
to wait, and he disappeared
through the cedar taking the flashlight
with him. Alone, peering into the dark
until I could no longer see or hear him,
a sudden noise, and a hulking shadow
rose up. I screamed, turned, and ran
into the gloom away from the hulk.
Away from Daddy.

Home, I crept quickly
up the stairs while Father raged
to Mama, She's no hunter;
leave her alone for a minute
to take a piss and she's scared
and running through those dark woods
imagining she saw a bear.
I'd never found her if she
didn't keep screaming.
His voice trembled.

Even now, though I can't forget,
I can scarcely speak it.

Nocturne
Michelle Menting

It's as if the moon begs me
to wonder: how eastern hemlock
still whispers against shadows
even now past midnight.
See them sweep? I see them,
demure branches of fine combs
blocking my view on this
needled path. I am lost.
I am lost and trying to find
your likeness wherever I go,
even on these insomniac strolls.
How unhealthy to yearn
for your existence, dear one,
sweet child that never was.
Babe of storybook, of fantasy,
of happy ending without stinging
swarm of subtext, no yelling
with decibel-fists. Dear fairytale,
dear wandering naïve—find me.
Hear my footfalls over the chorus
of frogs, over the flutter of thrush.
Let me curl you against this exhale
of dark, against these scarred ash
limbs battered by nor'easter storms.
Lay your nape into the crook
of my elbow while I rest
my bones on fungus birthing
from bark that still clings, still
holds too tightly to its own skin.

Why not blanket us both under
smoothcap moss, under velvet
forest floor? Dear changeling,
dear first of fir-bough loves, cast
your spell so that I, like you,
may forever sleep here too.

Hold It: Potty Talk for the Northern Maine Woods Camper

Chris Davis

Tell me, how long can you hold it?

When you were a kid traveling in the back seat of the station wagon, and you told your parents you needed to pee, the first thing they wanted to know was how long can you hold it?

Sitting in a movie theater, you feel the urge, but you don't want to miss an important plot point. You ask yourself: How long can I hold it?

You finally have the free time to peruse a local indie bookstore, and you get halfway through your favorite section. You have several promising hardcover candidates in your arms, and you begin to search for a good resting spot for them because there are two things you know. Number one, you can't take unpurchased merchandise into the lady's room. And number two, efficient employees may reshelve your stack while you're in the bathroom doing number one. Or number two. So you perform the "How long can I hold it?" dance in full view of other shopping customers and a handful of amused staff members. Sweat accumulates on your brow like you just accepted a dare from your old college buddies to take the Golden Fire Challenge at Buffalo Wild Wings.

Now, picture your childhood self in the loft of your family's camp. You're snug in your sleeping bag, trying to drift back to sleep, but a menacing urge persistently tickles your bladder, waking you up at irregular intervals. You open your eyes to get your bearings, but there is no light to help you recognize your surroundings. The power company hasn't established its presence yet in this pucker brush corner of the Northern Maine Woods.

The first step is to stand and assume the customary slouching posture to avoid hitting your head on the slanted ceiling. The second step is to stifle the cry of pain and rub your sore head when you bump your noggin anyway. Step three involves navigating to the loft ladder using only the plastic flashlight you got for your birthday with the nearly dead D-cell batteries.

As a young kid, you learned the all-important life skill of climbing down a steep ladder in bare feet with a bulky flashlight in one hand. You hope heaven smiles upon the human who invented the headlamp, but such fancy things were not widely available in the seventies. Crossing the linoleum floor, trying not to wake your family of slumbering campers, you reach the front door, slip on some camp shoes, and take a deep breath as you prepare to meet the ax murderer who is certainly waiting for you outside. The creaking floorboards of the front porch and the slap of the spring-loaded screen door announce to the boogeyman that you have entered his dark nighttime domain, and because you've procrastinated so long, your dash to the outhouse has become a desperate emergency.

You're not afraid of the dark. Who would be afraid of something they can't see? Or several somethings they can't see? Or many somethings they can't see? There are any number of somethings out there that you can't see. Not scary at all.

Pesky mosquitoes zero in on your infrared presence and buzz close to your ears, warning you the trip to the outhouse is too perilous. Owls ask each other rhetorical questions about what might bring a small human outside in the middle of the night. Tree leaves and the casual breeze conspire to shush the nocturnal creatures lurking in the woods. Tree roots sneakily stretch in your direction, trying to trip you as you blearily sleepwalk to the loo.

It's logical to assume that the pain of stubbing your toe during the daylight hours would feel equal to the pain of a nighttime toe stub. You don't know the science behind it, but it is a commonly accepted fact that getting hurt in the middle of the night is significantly more painful than the everyday walk-it-off type of pain experienced in the light of day. Your impulse to cry out is tempered by your mission to get to the outhouse and back quietly and safely, attracting as little attention as possible from things that go bump in the night.

You travel the orange pine needle carpet of a path, trying not to wake up too much so you can get back to sleep when this urinary nightmare is over. Your flashlight beam lands on the small wooden structure that promises relief, but not comfort. You pray the last visitor left enough paper on the roll.

Arriving at the outhouse, you reach up to open the squeaky door and are greeted by the acrid odor de toilette. Ice fishing augers, puffy orange life preservers, rusty saw blades, and sticky flypaper strips do not provide the ideal setting for squatting over an outhouse seat. You expose your bareness to the chill of the season and release your liquid burden into the dark hole while wondering what an ideal setting would be for such a thing. Maybe the soft flickering of a scented candle and some soothing elevator music? This is not the time to sit and ponder such luxurious accommodations. You pick up your flashlight and muster the moxie you'll need for the second half of this journey.

You return to the camp as your ninety-nine-cent cone of light bounces with each step. You're relieved and less frantic but still cautiously racing the bobcats, fishers, bears, skunks, raccoons, and Freddy Kruegers to the safety of a latching door. You console yourself with the assumption that they don't have the opposable thumbs necessary to open the camp's door. Then you remember that Freddy has fully functional thumbs, and you twist the doorknob locking mechanism just to be certain you and your loved ones are safe for the remainder of the night.

Your mother doesn't know you were recently introduced to the horror cinema genre at a friend's sleepover, and you will never feel safe in the woods again. Much like *Jaws* made movie buffs afraid to swim in the ocean, slasher movies made camping in nature not simply uncomfortable but life-threatening. Anyone not using the buddy system was asking for an unpleasant visit from a psychopath wielding a big knife.

For years, you've watched your grandmother head for the lake after dark with her flashlight and fishing pole. Her return with a steel pail full of eel was always a mystery, but now you begin to understand just what a badass your grammy was to brave the nighttime unknown and come back with a bucket of food.

You climb the ladder and settle back into your sleeping bag, zipping the sides for maximum protection and comfort. The warmth of your own body heat has waited for you to come back. You are safe. You are tired. You are free of distraction. Your sleep is quick to resume and, in your dreams, you relive memories of Christmas morning presents and warm chocolate chip cookies.

You wake up to the bright light of morning and the loons' cheerful announcement that a new day has started. This is when you learn that the older female family members simply take a small bundle of toilet tissue with them and squat beside the camp to avoid the trek to Spider Town USA in the dark of night. They casually mention this as they make their morning trip to the facilities and gather the used tissue bundles from the night before to dispose of them properly. You mentally slap your forehead and criticize yourself for not thinking of that while tucking the information away for your next foray of fright.

The possibility of Maine blueberry pancakes cooked in a cast-iron skillet accompanied by crispy, salty bacon erases all memory of the events you endured only a few hours before. You discover renewed happiness in the smell of a hearty camp breakfast. You draw the maple syrup close and hold it under your nose for a moment. You inhale the sweet fragrance. How long can you hold it inside you before you need to exhale and sniff another lungful?

How long can you hold the memory of this moment to reflect upon for years to come? How long can you hold true to the person you become when you connect with the natural world at this precious camp? How long can you hold onto the hope that you will come back and re-create this magic with your future family? How long can you hold your impatient heart still until the time when you grow to adulthood and decades later return to this sacred peaceful space with a realtor? How long can you hold onto the gratitude of having the opportunity to purchase this camp and bring it back into the family? How long can you hold this secret to yourself before you're ready to share it with the loved ones who cherish it the same way you always have?

The waiting is over. Exhale. Let go. You don't need to hold it anymore. Welcome home to the camp. Welcome home to yourself.

Man Climbing Katahdin

William Carpenter

After a final quarrel with his wife, after
they'd agreed it was all over, a man drove up
to Maine, to climb Katahdin. On the way, Haydn
was playing on the radio, but it seemed violent,
like a Prussian army marching upon his home
and taking his wife prisoner. He thought of her
in leg irons with a plate of lobster salad
just out of reach. He thought of her walking
towards it, reaching the end of her chain,
then falling back. He envied his friend Morris,
who lived with a student majoring in Health.
They spent Sundays in bed reading the *New York
Times*, and Morris had told him that her breasts
hid under the newspaper like turtles, so
the man thought about turtles as he started
up Katahdin. It felt as if his own body wore
a thick shell, making him climb slowly, making
him stop often to read the *Katahdin Guide*.
In 1843, it said, Henry Thoreau took the same
route up this mountain. As the man thought of
Thoreau, his shell seemed to burn off, and he
felt larger, he felt almost the same size
as Thoreau, and he imagined that Thoreau
gave him a hand at a place on the Knife Edge
where the snow was waist deep even in June, so
he could reach the summit and rest and look out
over the wilderness and the blue river snaking
to the sea. He wanted to say something to his
wife, he wanted to tell her that he'd climbed

the mountain with Thoreau, and from that height
the world looked different, it made sense, the way
music makes sense of feeling, or a book can make
sense of a human life. He wanted his wife to
be there on the summit, he wanted to show her
the alpine flowers, the log huts thousands
of feet below. He wanted to show her his hands,
how they were cut from the sharp granite, how
beneath the cuts there were the engraved lines
of the palms, like rivers; how some of these lines
were his—his wealth, his death—but one was hers,
and it would be easier to cut off his left hand
with his survival knife and leave it on
the Appalachian Trail than to erase that line.
He wanted to buy something at the campers' store,
even something stupid, like a shovel, and show up
in the middle of the night, holding the shovel
as a sign of peace, and say *this is a shovel,
this is from Thoreau*, so she would have to take it,
she'd have to let him in and give him coffee while
he told his story. She'd have to believe him, since
you have to believe what's there. It's all there is.

After Dark or Taking
After My Father

Patricia Smith Ranzoni

My senses of things change color
with northern earth beyond any known measure.

Beast-steps on our midnight roof waken me
with pleasure I see at dawn I invited, finding
the partridge guts drawn and wrapped yesterday
strewn in the ash where I'd return them next fire,
and in this way render praise for this natural life
found broken-necked under the ruptured screen.

The luck of knowing again bird feet in my fingers
dipping into the boil allowing the pull. Rip of feathers
from wings and tail. The smell. Creation in my hands
to arrange in order to honor.

The luck of a girlhood expecting this. Where
at the neck to slice. Where to disembowel.
How to reach into animal heat and what for.

How to enter gizzard. Peel out its mash.
Find its pure liver and nutlet heart touching yours—
woman chore.

Where to slit for the crop in anticipation,
your breath catching with revelation what unspoiled
food it last throated oh reddest red two berries
bright red and bites of leaves still green oh
what cure to have taken in.

Grapevines wild at the forest's edge have given away
their fruit living on in firelight, in flesh made of it
and partridge baked in their leaves. *I see my spirit free
and blow out any flown mistakenly into me.*

Squash-gold mushrooms multiplying
under the spruce require no promise nor the two dozen
turkeys bedding and roosting high in evergreen cover
out of reach of our shadows. Nor do I.
But I am only human.

Bath Towels and Deer Ticks:
A Maine Meet Cute

Dani Bannister

"Come to the North Woods," they said. "It'll be fun," they said. *They lied*. Every single one of my stupid friends who were married to nature-loving, bearded men. There was nothing *fun* about dodging bear poop and poison oak. An outdoorsy person, I was not. And yet, I let my gaggle of married friends convince me that renting a cabin in the North Woods of Maine would be just the thing I needed to recharge my batteries. So far, all the trip had done was remind me why I'd left the state as a teenager to begin with. There was nothing in Maine besides bugs in the summer, mud in the spring, and snow the rest of the year. No, thank you.

I'd asked my travel agent to pick something quiet and rustic that might be populated with single Paul Bunyan types. So far, it was only quiet and rustic. No men. *Figures*.

"How much higher up this mountain is this ridiculous cabin?" I asked the night sky.

An owl hooted in reply. *Helpful*.

With a dead cell battery and a GPS that got me lost multiple times, I was now faced with hoofing it up a "trail" I could barely make out by the moonlight to reach the cabin. If it wasn't so chilly, I'd sleep in the car. According to the travel agent, the cabin was just a few yards from the driveway. *More lies*.

That was when I saw it. A porch light. About two city blocks away. That unit of measurement I understood.

"About freaking time."

Tightening the straps of the only backpack I brought for the week, I took a deep breath. Rest and relaxation were minutes away. As much as I hated to admit it, my friends were right. I needed a break from city life. I needed to touch grass and breathe some fresh air. I was close to a mental breakdown. Work had been too much. I needed the getaway. But did the getaway have to be peppered with mosquitoes? At least I was getting my protein this trip.

By the time I made it to the cabin, I was sweaty and gross. My ponytail was falling out, and I was positive my mascara was nowhere near my lashes anymore. All I wanted to do was take a hot shower and go to bed. I could start my vacation in the morning. After copious amounts of coffee.

At the stairs, I noticed the large terracotta pot with the long-dead mums. According to my travel agent, Bekki—yes, with two *K*s and an *I* for some foolish reason—the key to the cabin would be under there.

"Bekki, I could kiss you."

I moved the pot and found the key. Thank God. After picking it up, I climbed the three steps to the small porch. The squeaky wooden screen door announced to all hungry animals that there was fresh meat to be devoured.

Just as I was sliding the key into the lock, the door suddenly swung open. With it came a bright yellow light from the lamps inside. Blinking several times to help my eyes adjust, I let out a gasp. Standing in front of me was the spitting image of Paul Bunyan, minus the ax and flannel. Well, minus *all* clothing. Save for a towel. He had on a towel. That was it.

"Oh, my God! I am so sorry. Bekki sent me to the wrong cabin," I said, looking again at the towel. That's when I realized I should turn around. Spinning quickly, I felt my cheeks flush. How humiliating. How did I get the wrong cabin? *Because it's the middle of the night, you can't see shit, and Bekki does not leave good instructions.*

"Bekki? Not Bekki Turner by chance?" the man asked.

"Um, yeah. Do you know her?"

He let out a large sigh. "Unfortunately. She's my sister. And this is my cabin. Let me guess, you're some down-on-her-luck city girl looking for an escape from it all?"

I was instantly annoyed that he'd labeled me so quickly. "I wouldn't say I am down on my luck. I make damn good money. And I'm not a 'girl.' I'm a woman. I know you probably don't see a lot of those around here walking outside with the moose and the deer."

"She sent a feisty one this time." He laughed.

At that, I turned. "*This time?*"

"I love my sister. Honestly. But she tends to play matchmaker. She sends every *woman* looking for a getaway to Maine to my cabin and then conveniently *forgets* to tell me she's rented out the family cabin for the week. Funny how she only forgets when I'm here for the month."

This was a botched setup?

"Well, that's awesome. I only flew eight hours, drove three, and now have no battery left on my cell and no place to sleep." That was when a large clap of thunder hit. Followed by the sounds of raindrops. "And now it's raining. This is my life."

Sighing, I pushed the hair off my face to head back to the car. Assuming I could find it again. I'd have to murder Bekki in the morning. Once I found a charger.

"Where are you going?" the man asked.

"To my car. There must be a hotel somewhere near here."

"There isn't. You're kind of in the middle of nowhere."

I turned around and gestured. "I hadn't noticed." The rain started to come down harder, landing in big, fat, cold drops on my face.

"Come inside. I'm not going to leave you out in the woods in a rainstorm."

"Thanks, but I don't know you from Adam, so ..."

He reached out a hand. "Name's Paul."

"Of course it is," I muttered. "I'm Sophia."

"Nice to meet you, Sophia. Now, will you come inside and get warm? If it would help, I could put on some pants."

Paul had jokes. Serial killers weren't funny. Maybe I wouldn't die if I accepted his offer. "Toss on a shirt and give me access to a phone charger, and you might have yourself a deal," I countered.

"The shirt I can do. The charger, I'm afraid I can't help you with. I don't bring my phone when I come out here."

"No phone?" I gasped. "What do you do out here for a month without a phone?"

He let out a deep belly laugh. "I read. Hike, kayak, and sip coffee on the porch."

"Huh. I planned to lie in bed all week, eat potato chips, and doom scroll."

"Some vacation."

"You relax your way. I relax mine."

Another loud clap of thunder, this time with a huge bolt of lightning.

"Right. Time for you to find those pants."

Paul opened the door wider. I would either have a wild story to tell my girlfriends or end up on the first page of the news as: *City woman found dead in the woods.* Either way, it would be a killer story.

The cabin was just like you would imagine the inside of a Maine cabin in the middle of the woods. Light-colored wood everywhere. Pine? Oak? I don't know wood. Whatever it was, it was literally everywhere. The floors were wood; the walls were wood. The doors, obviously, were wood. The ceiling, wood. The only things not made of wood were the appliances that were older than my mother.

"Is it wise to have a woodstove going when the whole place is literal kindling?" I asked as Paul disappeared into what I presumed was his bedroom. One could only assume there was more wood in there.

"As long as we keep the fire inside the stove, we should be good," he yelled.

"That's comforting," I mumbled, plopping my bag down onto the couch that had an afghan on it remarkably similar to the one my grandmother had made—brown, orange, and yellow squares, all crocheted together to make one vomit-covered monstrosity. Was there no other colored yarn in the seventies?

Paul came out a moment later with jeans (pity) and a—you guessed it—red button-up flannel that was undone one button too many.

"Can I get you a cup of coffee or a glass of wine? Water?"

"Wine? Yes, please. It's been a hell of a day. I forgot how far away everything is here."

"Not your first time in Maine then?" he asked, opening the wood cabinets and pulling out two empty glasses.

"Unfortunately not. I was born here but left after I graduated high school. It's funny. I left because I thought Orono—that's where I'm from—was stifling. Compared to San Fran, it's laughable."

Paul brought over the glasses filled to the brim with something red. I didn't even care what. I took a deep guzzle, only mildly turned off by the tannins.

"Did you want to use the bathroom? To freshen up?" he asked. He gestured to my face, which told me I must look like utter shit. "And maybe check for ticks."

"I should check for ticks?" I asked, putting my glass down. I felt itchy all of a sudden.

Paul shrugged. "I usually spray my clothes with a repellant or put a layer of double-sided tape around the cuffs of my pants when I hike up here. There are always at least two or three stuck there. Might be a good idea to check."

"Jesus H. Christ," I said, darting off the couch. "Where's the bathroom?"

"First door on the right," he said. She heard him chuckling softly as she bolted for the room.

To tell you I never stripped down to my birthday suit faster in my life would be an understatement. I scanned my legs, which, because they were freshly shaven, were easy to scan. God forbid if I had had a few days of growth. I might never see anything crawling around on me.

"Check between your toes, armpits, and, um, in any cracks or crevices," he said from the other side of the door. "They like the dark."

I froze where I stood inside the world's tiniest bathroom. "I could have ticks in my ass cheeks?"

He did his best to stifle a laugh, but I heard it loud and clear. "Technically, yes. But I do have a tick-picker. If you find any, let me know. You don't want to take them off by hand. You could crush them, and their guts spill out, and well, that's how Lyme happens."

"Gross. If I find a tick on me, do me a solid and just toss me into that wood-stove. Deal?"

"Why don't we cross that bridge when we get to it?"

I went back to checking, almost not daring to look. That was when I realized I couldn't actually *see* my butt. Not without several hand mirrors and creative yoga poses to get into a position to see inside the crevices in that area. Still, I had to try.

Standing on the toilet, I turned around and tried to bend and see in the small mirror what I could see in this cramped, poorly lit room. *Sophia, you're being dramatic. There aren't any ticks on you—*

"Tick!" I shrieked. "Paul! Help! I have a tick on me. Ahhh!" I started to shake my limbs as though that would remove the thing from the inside of my ass cheek. "What do I do?"

Before I could hyperventilate, the door opened, and Paul came in, tick-picker in hand. One problem: I was still buck-naked.

"Oh, God! Sorry, sorry!" He spun around, but it was too late. He'd seen all there was to see. "I should have knocked," he continued. "I didn't know you were naked."

"It's fine. Just get it off me. Please!" I am not proud of the screeches that came out of me. I was acting like a prepubescent child, but the idea of a bug burrowing into my butt sent shivers of disgust down my body. I didn't care how naked I was if it meant this thing got off my skin faster.

"Come into my bedroom. Lie on the bed."

I frowned. "You'd like that, wouldn't you?"

"The light is better there. Besides, the two of us can't exactly fit in this space."

It was true. Our bodies were practically touching. Which wasn't helping matters in the slightest. Was it possible to be disgusted and turned on at the same time? Because I totally was.

Huffing, I grabbed my shirt from off the floor and covered my front. Then, as quickly as I could, I marched my naked butt to his bedroom. As predicted, his room was wall-to-wall wood. Collapsing face-first onto his bed, I let out a yowl of disgust.

"You good?" Paul asked.

"Tick. Ass. Now," I yelled into the bed.

I heard his deep chuckle again as he climbed onto the bed. "Okay, where is it?"

Tilting my head, I pointed at my left cheek. "It's right there? Can't you see it? Oh, God, you don't think it climbed inside already, do you?"

"You mean this?" He pointed to the very spot.

"Yes! Get it off me. Don't poke it! You said not to poke at it!"

"Sophia, um, I don't know how to tell you this, but that's not a tick. It's a mole. A harmless, normal mole."

"That's a mole?" I twisted to see, but I couldn't. I was not that flexible. Instead, I reached a finger down to feel and confirm that it was not a bug.

"I have a mole on my ass?"

"You do. But, no tick. You're safe."

"While also naked in a stranger's bed. Only me." I sighed, collapsing back onto the bed.

"We're not strangers. You're Sophia, and I'm Paul."

"Hi."

His laugh shook the bed. "Hi. Welcome to the Maine North Woods, Sophia."

And that is the day I met your father and, coincidentally, the night you were conceived.

Wildcat
Matt Bernier

If not for tracks in snow
what is improbable in dark
would be impossible in light;

a bobcat has sauntered
around a vernal pool
after an April storm,

falling trees only
making sounds for the
feline's tufted ears;

she prefers striding over
hoar frost for its swift
morning disappearance,

but she meets this new
precipitation where it is,
leaving soft impressions

on her nocturnal rounds,
and I follow, without pursuit,
through a stand of red cedars,

and here where she walks
I will let her walk,

and here where she gallops
I will let her gallop,

and here where she jumps
I will let her jump,

until one day I will discover
claw marks on a sugar maple
with weeping sap,

and will realize, only then,
that her territorial rounds
end where they start;

under a new moon's murk,
like the harsh darkness
between constellations,

she will reach up, purring,
scratching to finally claim
what is rightfully sweet.

The Path
Catherine J.S. Lee

In the clearing
at the grove where our family
held its three-day reunion,
we sat on plank benches
around the evening campfire.
Smoke and sparks and laughter
rose on the crisp autumn air
as our grandfathers told stories
of long-ago adventures
in northern fields and forests.

An ice-white moon
rose in the star-speckled sky,
but in the grove, among the tall pines,
the bushy spruces,
the stately, ghostly birches,
moonbeams fell like shards of mirrors
through the leaves and needled branches,
a scattered radiance
no match for the velvet darkness
beneath the trees.

Invariably and inevitably,
full-up on lemonade or soda pop,
one by one we kids would hear
the call of the outhouse.
The outhouse!
Deeper into the woods
where its reek could not offend,

it sat at the end of a long path
up the slope and through the thicker trees,
where the campfire cast no light
and shadows reigned.

To ask for company on the walk
was to admit a lack of courage,
but in this I was immune
to the opinions of cousins.
"Mummy, come with me," I'd whisper,
for being tagged a scaredy-cat
was nothing compared to my seven-year-old self
getting carried off by something in the woods.
"Go on," she'd tell me. "You'll be fine."
Disappointed and frightened,
I'd sit and fidget till I could wait no longer,
and then I'd run my fastest up the hill.

Later, I learned there was
nothing that would harm me
here in these Maine woods.
Still later, I began to understand
my mother's lesson—
in doing what I feared,
I began to walk the path
to finding courage.

Not Deer in Maine?

Christopher Packard

Not Deer /nät dir/ (noun) A dangerous nocturnal creature of the eastern United States that resembles a white-tailed deer but with unsettling features and predatory behaviors.

White-tailed deer (*Odocoileus virginianus*) are one of the most familiar members of Maine's fauna. These gentle forest herbivores are often seen as a symbol of idyllic wilderness—the very embodiment of the forest. But while deer are found throughout Maine, they are rarest in the North Woods. They are most common in southern and central Maine, where the winters are less harsh and more fields are found. Deer are picky eaters and depend on lots of nonwoody plants to support them. In the North Woods, especially where the trees are not recently lumbered, winter can be deadly hard for them. Maine's many skilled hunters know that deer can be like ghosts of the forest, remaining unseen unless you know how to look for them. They are liminal creatures, crepuscular—most active around dawn and dusk and rarely seen at other times. But they are creatures of habit following the same paths and patterns day after day unless people are about, and then lying low and becoming more active at night when they will not be disturbed.

Maine is known for its woods and wildlife. It has more black bears and moose than any of the other lower forty-eight states, yet many visitors will never see a black bear (*Ursus americanus*) or a moose (*Alces alces*). For most, the deer will be the only large animal they will see because deer like the openings and roadsides that humans create.

The most famous deer in the world, Walt Disney's Bambi, was born in the Maine woods. One of the key lead animation designers for the 1943 motion picture was Maurice "Jake" Day, a native of Maine. He frequented the Katahdin region and, with Walt's blessing, based the designs for the movie on this area after collecting volumes of research footage there. The real Bambi was an orphaned fawn transported from Maine to California for the Disney animators to base their drawings on. Ironically, the movie is strongly antihunting. It romantically anthropomorphizes the animals and turns man into a monster. This sentiment certainly caused it to be less than popular with many of the residents of the very state where it was set. In 1943 at least, Maine residents, many of them hunters, were certain Bambi was not the deer that *they* knew in the Maine woods.

Interestingly, deer were not always abundant in the state. Wildlife biologists believe that before the arrival of Europeans in the 1600s, the Maine deer herd was small and largely restricted to the southern coast. With colonization came agricultural clearings, lumbering, and the extermination of predators. These actions transformed the landscape into one more suitable for white-tailed deer, who thrive in habitats that are a patchwork of fields, edges, and dense canopy cover. So perhaps the hunters were correct; for deer, humans and their guns were not monsters, but rather the agents of habitat expansion.

Lately, rumors of a new monster—the Not Deer—have been spreading across Maine. These Not Deer are just what their name implies: they are not deer. At first glance, they look like deer, but something seems off. Their proportions are wrong, their coats are rough, and their eyes face forward like a predator. And unlike deer, Not Deer have no fear of humans, sometimes inching closer and closer, as if stalking them—something a prey species like deer definitely shouldn't do. They move in an odd, uncomfortable way with jerky movements, and they make whistles and clicks. If you come across a Not Deer, it's best to back away, go inside if possible, and forget what you saw.

These folk cryptids are a recent arrival to the United States, with mentions of them first appearing on the blogging site Tumblr in 2019 and spreading rapidly via the internet and word of mouth. Even so, they are not well-known by hunters and other outdoor enthusiasts. It's unclear if Not Deer exist in Maine, as sightings have mostly been reported in the Southern Appalachians. However, things change in Maine, and it's best to be prepared should these creatures appear in our woods.

Many people hypothesize that Not Deer may be an observation of deer infected with chronic wasting disease (CWD), the so-called zombie deer disease. CWD is caused by a prion and is similar to mad cow disease. Prions are virus-like, self-replicating proteins that induce neurological disorders by causing neural proteins in the brain to refold. Infected deer exhibit dramatic weight loss, stumbling, blank expressions, loss of fear of humans, and general neurological degeneration. This disease has not been detected in Maine or New England but is present in the

Southern Appalachians and throughout the Midwest, where it began spreading in the 1970s from a captive deer population.

CWD is an environmentally contagious disease that infects deer, moose, elk, and caribou, and it invariably leads to the death of those infected. The U.S. Centers for Disease Control and Prevention recommends against consuming or coming into contact with infected deer or their body fluids. Infected deer are concerning, but even those that appear zombie-like are not monsters; they are simply sick animals.

Nevertheless, deer do affect the North Woods in some unexpected ways. Before deer were widespread, and even through the 1800s, moose and woodland caribou (*Rangifer tarandus caribou*) were the undisputed dominant antlered animals of the North Woods. Today, moose still exist, but despite the many moose crossing signs on I-95 and the hopes of tourists, they are seldom seen in the southern or central parts of the state. This is largely due to the higher deer densities in those areas and the spread of a non-CWD disease among them.

White-tailed deer are the primary host of brain worm (*Parelaphostrongylus tenuis*), a nematode parasite. They become infected by accidentally consuming a slug or snail that carries the worm's larvae. The consumed larvae travel along the deer's nerves to the brain, where they mature and lay eggs in the animal's bloodstream. The eggs hatch into larvae that are excreted in the deer's feces. When slugs and snails feed on the infected feces, they become hosts, thus perpetuating the cycle. This process is harmless to the deer, but in moose, the brain worms and their eggs become lodged in the brain, causing weight loss, stumbling, circling, loss of fear of humans, and overall neurological degeneration that leads to death. In the North Woods, where deer densities are lowest, moose only occasionally become infected with brain worms, but where deer are common, they easily become infected and die. So, where there are deer, there are *not moose*.

Although they are no longer present, woodland caribou were once plentiful in Maine's North Woods, with some estimates placing their population in the hundreds of thousands. These herds were decimated by professional market hunters who shot entire herds and shipped them off to cities for sale as meat. Habitat alteration also deeply affected caribou populations. These animals require large areas of mature, undisturbed forests to thrive, and widespread lumbering has altered that habitat in ways that persist to this day. This change to younger regenerating forests ironically benefited both moose and deer populations. In

1963 and 1993, the State of Maine reintroduced caribou to the state. Both times, they were released in the Katahdin area, and both times, all individuals died or migrated out of the area—with the deaths primarily attributed to brain worm infection. So, like the moose, where there are deer, there are *not caribou*.

While this relationship between deer, moose, and caribou may be news to most Maine residents and has only been understood by biologists in the past few decades, it has long been known to the Indigenous peoples of Maine. In a 1938 *Journal of Mammalogy* article titled "Late Records of Caribou in Maine," wildlife biologist Ralph Palmer offhandedly notes what likely seemed to him a quaint native hypothesis: "The Penobscot explanation for why there are no caribou is that the deer 'polluted' the woods and thus drove their relatives away." So again, where there are deer, there are *not caribou*.

But the deer aren't the monsters; they are just navigating their way through a changing world. And the sport hunters in *Bambi* aren't the monsters either. It's our disconnection from the natural world and our lack of understanding of the wide-ranging effects of our actions that lead us to see the world as an endless resource to exploit without consequence. Maine's North Woods may have the lowest human population density east of the Mississippi, the largest forest in the contiguous United States, and the darkest night skies comparable to none, but even it is not immune to the impacts of human activity and climate change.

Our fear is misplaced. Rather than being scared of Not Deer in the woods, we should be scared that we are so out of touch with the ways of the natural world that we don't see or care about the harm we do. We should be scared that we've forgotten how to live in harmony with the Earth and that we are so disconnected, we have become Not Human.

The 100-Mile Wilderness
Emily M. Leonard

"Come on, kids, let's not keep your father waiting. You know he hates that," Mom bellowed from the kitchen as she packed the remaining items into her bags. My brother and I excitedly ran from one room to the next in the old Victorian home, making sure we had what we wanted.

We hadn't seen Dad in a week. Mom held down the home front with seven kids while Dad spent weekdays at the logging camp deep in the North Maine Woods off the Katahdin Iron Works Road. I never knew Katahdin Iron Works was the name until I was an adult. As a kid, I just remembered it being so very far from home.

Of the seven kids, Buddy and I were the only two children going to see Dad. The others were several years older and could be left on their own. Buddy and I were still in elementary school and needed adult supervision.

Since it was Friday, the other lumberjacks were heading home to be with their own families for the weekend, freeing up the community bunks. Mom convinced us that spending time at the old cabin without electricity, plumbing, or private bedrooms was a vacation. What did we know? We were kids and easily pleased, but we were also self-sufficient little tykes. Just get us to the woods, and we could entertain ourselves for hours. Looking back, I now realize that was the only kind of vacation my parents could afford.

Spending the weekends with Dad at the lumberjack camp and sitting on the cabin porch in the evenings counting stars as the owls hooted sparked my love for the wilderness. The quietness of the night enveloped us. Talking was scant. Mom knitted while puffs of white smoke from a cigarette hung in the air around Dad like a halo in the glow of the moon. At the time, I was too young to understand the gem called the North Maine Woods. I just knew I loved it there. After Mom and Dad tucked my brother and me in our bunks, I would sink my head into the pillow as the musty smell of decades-old sawdust, oil, and sweat from hardworking men wafted around me. As loud as sirens piercing the cabin walls, the chirps and croaks of crickets and frogs serenaded me to sleep.

On some weekends, the moon shined so brightly through the windows that it woke me in the middle of the night like a beacon calling me outside. One such night, I saw Dad gazing out through the smoke-filmed pane, and I went to him. He lifted me so I had a better view, and my eyes widened as I saw a doe and her two fawns feeding on the grass. If it had been autumn, one of them may have become breakfast, but that night, we watched in silence as the three docile animals munched on their greens.

My childhood memories are dotted with vacations spent at the Katahdin Iron Works lumberjack camp. As I grew, family outings changed, but one theme ran through them all—the Maine woods.

By the time I was in junior high, Dad no longer worked at the lumberjack camp. His days cutting wood slowly decreased, but for extra income, he still helped his friend Mr. Michaud on occasion. Dad spent many weekends cutting trees. I tagged along, not to work but just to be with him and to smell the fresh-cut cedar, hemlock, and pine.

Our aging F-150 pickup truck rattled along the washboard dirt road, and layers of dust collected on the seats, dashboard, and my arm as I floated my fingers through the summer air out the open window. The red-and-white, grease-stained Playmate cooler was nestled in the truck's bed between a chainsaw and other tools. Baking in the sun, the cooler contained our bologna sandwiches but no ice and acted more like an oven than a food-safety device.

We arrived at the logging lay-down yard and immediately began getting ready for the task at hand—cutting wood. I jumped into the back of the truck, handed the tools to Dad, and then hopped back out. Dad always started the day by sharpening his saw. This was painful for me. I helped steady the machine on the tailgate as he used a round metal file to grind any burrs and nicks from the chainsaw's teeth.

Scrinch! SCRinncchh!! SCRINNNCCHHH!!! With each swipe of the metal file against the metal blade, my entire being cringed. I not only disliked the sound, but I also seemed to feel the abrasiveness throughout my body. Even my teeth hurt with each pass. The filing motion made fingernails on a chalkboard seem relaxing. But I couldn't say anything. My dad, a retired infantry first sergeant, never allowed weakness or excuses. You did what needed to be done without complaining.

Surviving the first task of the day, I was free to wander the woods until it was time to eat our slimy-warm bologna sandwiches. What most might consider disgusting seemed like five-star cuisine as Dad and I sat on a log deep in the Maine woods, eating our lunch. What more could a girl want?

The second part of the day went like the first part, beginning again with the sharpening of the saw. Surviving round two, I went back to exploring as Dad went back to work. One of my favorite pastimes was identifying as many varieties of scat and animal tracks as I could—skills I am still fascinated with.

After a long, hard day's work (for Dad), we reloaded the Ford with the gear and several pieces of wood to be burned that winter, which added a few more dents and scratches to the truck's character. This time, I climbed in the back for an open-air ride. I sat sidesaddle on the right wheel well. I again let my right arm float through the air. In areas where the alders grew closer to the road, I held my arm out straight so my palm could give high-fives to the leaves.

The day was no longer bright and sunny; the sun had begun its journey downward, casting shadows through the trees. The tickling sensation of leaves teasing my palm and fingers as the truck sped along the dirt road gave way to sharp, knife-like stinging. Due to the shadows, I did not see the thorns hiding within the alders. I yanked my arm back into the safety of the truck bed. My palm looked like a dog's nose that had inspected a porcupine a little too closely. Thankfully, it was only raspberry briars and not a thorny plum tree. The pain was enough, though, for me to rap on the truck window, asking Dad to stop so I could ride in the cab with him.

On several occasions, Dad worked extra-long hours, and dusk would overtake us before we exited the woods. Those were my favorite days. I loved riding in a vehicle in the woods at night when animals were more active, escaping the day's heat. Moths and bats fluttered in the headlights. Deer fed in open areas. Raccoons combed the sides of the roads, looking for anything to feast on. Many times, we followed a moose down the road. If it was a rainy night, we saw tiny frogs in a mass. That's why we also carried an empty covered bucket. I was tasked with catching the leapers as well as any night crawlers who were escaping their flooded channels to sell as bait back home in our bait and tackle shop.

There was something thrilling about seeing the glowing eyes of an animal reflecting the truck's headlights back to us. Two dots at the far reaches of the beams were all that could be seen. Instinctually, Dad gently applied the brakes. As the truck approached, bit by bit, the shape of the animal emerged from the darkness in the ever-increasing strength of the headlights as we rolled closer. It was a game to see who could guess the species first. More times than not, Dad won.

During my high school years, I continued to spend time in the woods with Dad when academia or sports allowed. For fun, Dad and I drove the back roads at night to see a deer. Little did I know there was a deeper need for doing this back then. Money was still tight on his small, retired-army income; he fed us steak as often as he could. With that secret held tight, Dad ensured these nighttime outings were fun.

Springtime meant it was smelting season. We would return to the Maine woods at night, to the "hidden" spot that quickly became too crowded to fish. I didn't mind. I enjoyed just being there with Dad, but he was focused on catching our limit to sell in the shop. I spent the time gazing at the stars, listening to the owls, and making fun of the drunks who fell into the stream.

Spending the night at a friend's hunting camp became yet another affordable vacation during the annual deer hunting season. After a hearty breakfast, whoever was participating in the day's hunt went to their respective trail and stand. No longer needing adult supervision, I soon became skilled at solo hunting and walked to my own stand.

I liked departing from camp in the morning under the cover of darkness as the forest still slept. I would climb to my perch as the sun carved silhouettes of trees through the darkness, signaling that I could legally load my gun. I wasn't so fond of the afternoon hunt. Then, everything took place in reverse. I would return to my stand in daylight, where I stayed until legal hours were over. Unload. Then, meet back at the truck.

Although I enjoyed driving through the woods at night, I didn't like walking out alone with an empty gun after dark. Headlamps were a luxury we didn't have. Guided by what little rays still glowed through the trees, I dreaded the dark and scary walk. Everything seemed bigger. The noises louder. The unseen more terrifying. But I did it because that's what I was told to do.

College years and starting a family separated me from the North Maine Woods. More than twenty years would pass before I returned. We brought the kids back for a day-vacation hike and swim at Gulf Hagas on the Katahdin Iron Works Road. It wasn't until that day I realized that was where I used to go visit Dad when he worked in the woods. What seemed like a long journey as a child turned out to be a short ninety-minute ride as an adult. That revelation brought back fond memories of why I love the woods so.

Another six years passed before I returned to those forests. This time, it was at the end of my Appalachian Trail thru-hike when I was a forty-nine-year-old empty-nester. No longer fearing the woods at night, I developed a love for the serenity and peacefulness nighttime brings to my soul—except for one terrifying night partway through my hike of the 100-Mile Wilderness section in the North Maine Woods.

Since the White Mountains in New Hampshire, I had been hiking with two other gals my age who were not from Maine. At the end of the day, Bruce, my husband, met us with fresh sandwiches and a resupply. He left, and then my hiking buddies and I retired to our tents. I relaxed to the forest sounds, and just before drifting off, I heard it approaching. All those years in the woods with Dad had taught me to identify not only scat and tracks but also different noises. This noise was big, and it was headed straight for me!

Fearing being trampled on as I lay on my air mattress, I sat up. The crinkling noise scared the beast and it took off like nobody's business, crashing and trashing out of the woods onto the logging road. After all the commotion, one of my friends yelled from her tent, "Black Bear!"—my trail name. "What the hell was that?"

Narrowly escaping danger, I jokingly replied, "That, my friend, was your Maine moose!"

Two years passed, and I found myself back in the 100-Mile Wilderness on my second Appalachian Trail thru-hike. The Maine woods kept calling me back, but this time, for healing. Before I could finish my second hike, Dad passed away. I left the trail to be with him in his final moments. After his death and services, I returned to finish my hike. I soon found myself in the same woods he had taken me as a young child, the place we vacationed because it was all we could afford. Those woods were a source of joy in my childhood and throughout my growing years. Now, as an adult, they have become a source of healing when life becomes overwhelming.

The Maine woods are teeming with life, and while treasures are visible when the sun is high, the true beauty emerges under the cover of darkness. Yes, they are scarier in the dark. Yes, things are louder. Yes, it is lonelier. But when you manage that rampant, fearful imagination of *false evidence appearing real* and allow your soul to rest, you discover the healing powers of quietness and the beauty of darkness. You can recline in the solitude of your thoughts, clearing your mind of clutter and seeing how great things really are.

The shadows that seemed so big when I was a child create a canvas blocking out all distractions in my adultness. The noises that seemed so loud then sharpen my senses today. The unseen that seemed so terrifying in my youth now piques my curiosity. The nocturnal nature of the Maine woods grasps my being like a spell.

When I am tired. When my heart aches. When I am depressed. When I long for Dad or any other type of comfort, it isn't a fancy, expensive European trip or cruise that I plan for. Rather, I pack my bag and some boring sandwiches and head for the North Maine Woods.

Alone in the Woods

J.D. Mankowski

A man sits alone in the woods. He knows he is alone because he has neither seen nor heard anybody else come near. A dense canopy blocks out any view of the heavens. Light from a campfire illuminates the area. The Man has claimed it as his own. He believes it is his own because he tells himself so.

The animals in the woods do not approach; the Man smells of iron to them. They know the fire cannot ever truly be controlled. It is dangerous, like so many other things the Man has carried into the woods with him. To fight the dark with everlasting daylight is unnatural—trivial even—because the sun always rises again when it's supposed to. The animals do not tell the Man this. They know their warnings are useless. He does not remember the Language.

The Man's ignorance is why the trees around him speak freely, why they mock him. They have watched the Man grow taller with age but not wiser. It is so very human nowadays to not put down roots and learn. It is so very human instead to travel like samaras caught on a strong wind—to spin and fall as far away from home as possible. To never seed because the environment they come upon is somehow always wrong. Only the tree's laughter catches the Man's attention. Their creaking causes the hairs on the Man's neck to stand up on end.

The Man fears the woods at night. Human stories have encouraged it. Monstrous attacks, nature's wrath, the unpredictable chaos that threatens his delicate mortal existence. The Man cannot control what he cannot see. The Man feels vulnerable. The spear by his side gives him comfort.

The animals do not approach; they know what the Man will do with his spear if they draw too close. They also know that Black Bear, the animal the Man fears most, is far away. Black Bear does not care for him. There are better things to eat than the Man, like berries, nuts, and roots. Gray Wolf is another animal the Man fears, which the animals find laughable. Gray Wolf has not inhabited these woods in over a century. Coyote, Lynx, Bobcat, and Cougar are definitely present, but they prefer to chase their meals. The Man no longer runs.

Refuses to root. Refuses to run; this truth causes the trees to creak again. The Man does not understand the joke. He takes up his spear and tries to discern the dangers he knows for certain are lurking in the shadows.

The Man is alone in the woods. He knows he is alone because he has neither seen nor heard anybody else come near. So, it is a surprise to him when a harmless elder steps out of the darkness and into the light of his fire.

The Elder appears with a quiet dignity, embodying the essence of experience. Each step taken is deliberate yet unhurried, as if in tune with the rhythm of the woods itself. The Elder's face is weathered, etched with the lines of a life well-lived. Their eyes are sharp and observant. Clad in simple garments of earthy tones, the Elder blends seamlessly with the surroundings, their presence as natural as the wind.

The Elder smiles warmly, knowing how the Man is feeling. The Man cannot be alone now that they are there in the firelight together. The Elder does not speak but sits down when the Man gestures toward a space he is willing to share. There is comfort in the company. The Elder watches the Man loosen his grip on his spear.

All of life's wisdom sits beside the Man like an open book, but the Man chooses to watch the shadows instead. The Elder does not scold him but sits patiently and looks toward the divide between the woods and the light. When the wind passes over the Man's fire, it scatters portions of the shadows for an instant, and in that instant, the Elder can spot the animals.

Eastern Gray Squirrel is the most curious. The Elder finds it scavenging near the Man's discarded food scraps. It doesn't matter if the Man builds a shelter or an entire city; it will always be nearby.

Red-backed Vole scurries along the edge of the campfire's glow, its tiny paws barely making a sound as it searches for fallen seeds and scattered crumbs. Pausing briefly to listen for any real signs of danger, Vole takes quick, darting movements in and out of the underbrush. Despite the warmth of the fire, Vole remains vigilant, ever aware of the Man and his spear ... of Fox ... and of Hawk.

Up in the trees, Saw-whet Owl, Raven, Black-capped Chickadee, and Spruce Grouse watch. If the trees of these woods ever had eyes, they were gifted to these birds who now look down on the Man and the Elder.

The Elder can converse with any of them if the opportunity arises. The Elder's left pocket is full of seeds. The right pocket holds a set of hand-carved bird calls. The Elder lost the complete Language long ago. All they know now is based on the time they've dedicated to relearning. They would teach the Man all they knew if the Man asked, if he valued such knowledge.

The Man grows impatient with the Elder's silence. If they won't take up a spear or speak or gather or hunt, if they won't help him survive the night, why did they come into the woods? The Man doesn't ask this question. Instead, he assumes the Elder was simply lost and, now having been found, will be content to wait until dawn.

The trees have stopped mocking the Man to converse with the Elder instead. The Elder nods along to the way they bend their branches. The Elder listens to their stories. When the wind shakes their leaves, the Elder sighs deeply, closing their eyes to understand more. The Elder and the trees breathe as one. The trees appreciate the Elder because they approach without wanting. They do not seek shade, bark, wood, fruit, or the ground they're rooted in. The Elder does not claim ownership of them. Where the Man grows tall without wisdom, the Elder droops under the weight of it. The trees tell the Elder that they look more and more like Old Black Willow. The Elder laughs.

The Man means to snap at the Elder. Any noise might welcome danger closer. But a strong wind pushes through the woods and dampens the firelight. When it recovers with the assistance of more logs, the Man discovers that the Elder has gone.

The Man sits alone in the woods. He believes he has always been alone because he neither saw nor heard the Elder get up to leave. A figment of his imagination played tricks on him. The campfire struggles to preserve the small space of woods he has claimed as his own. It remains his own because he continues to tell himself so.

The animals creep closer as the burning logs sizzle and hiss. They know the Man adds wet wood. The trees drop more of their green branches and sticks for fun. The Man adds it to his dying fire. Smoke billows upward in a burly column of white. It chokes out what little light remains. Orange embers blink, then fade. The woods fall silent.

The Man panics. He doesn't know where to aim his spear. He cannot hear if danger approaches. The Man stands in the woods at night. He is alone. He is afraid.

A child's cackle echoes behind him. The Man spins around, startled. Someone pokes him. He thrusts his spear in the dark. The laughter sounds again, only this time from somewhere high up in the trees. The Man backs up blindly, jabbing his spear in every direction. The laughter haunts him as if born from the shadows.

Tree branches snap and fall all around him. Animals chime in with caws and chirps and calls of their own. The Man screams. The laughter stops.

Moonlight pierces through a large opening made in the canopy and illuminates the forest floor. A small child, no older than four or five, basks in the middle of the ethereal light. Their tousled hair, the color of midnight, frames their face in wild curls that seem to catch the light and reflect it back in a thousand hues. Clad in simple garments woven from leaves and vines, the Child exudes a sense of purity that is both familiar and mysterious. The Child looks at the Man while sitting atop Gray Wolf. Cupped in their hands is Deer Mouse. Perched on their right shoulder is Owl. Snake crowns their head. The Man does not believe his eyes. He calls out to the Child if only to prove himself still sane—if only to prove that he has not fallen prey to the games of his fear-fueled imagination. Tricks of the woods at night.

The Child ignores him and looks up toward the sky. The Man calls out again. He is unwilling to lower his spear, for while the Child may be harmless, Gray Wolf is not.

Deer Mouse disagrees with the Man's thoughts and proves it by leaving the Child's cupped hands to sit comfortably atop Gray Wolf's head.

The Child and Snake look at the Man. The Man becomes acutely aware that he is now standing in the shadows. That his campsite in the woods is now occupied by someone other than him, something other than him.

Owl takes flight out of the opening of the canopy. The Child slides off Gray Wolf. The Man calls out for a third time. In reply, the Child and Gray Wolf howl up toward the heavens. When the Man does not follow suit, the Child stops and looks at him. Gray Wolf howls again; its independent song reverberates in the Man's chest. The Child points upward. When Gray Wolf howls for a third time, he joins in again.

The Man does not howl, but he tilts his head back, allowing his eyes to trace the arc of the Milky Way as it stretches across the night sky. With each passing moment, he becomes more familiar with the dynamic interplay of celestial bodies, their movements choreographed by the inexorable forces of gravity and motion. The galaxy spirals with its arms reaching outward—stars, planets, and nebulae whirl around its central core. The woods at night rise to meet it. The Man's sense of self is scrambled. His fear is instantly eradicated by a rhapsodic understanding that extends beyond the bones that support, the skin that dresses, the memories and thoughts that conceive him. The Man bursts forth with awe.

The Child speaks, and the Man remembers in that moment how to hear the Language.

The Man stands in the woods at night. He knows he is not alone because he has never been alone. He is part of something greater.

Medwaymorphosis
Michael G. Dunn

Sophia struggled to whisper, and gasping breaths hugged her lungs. "Please tell me I'm not crazy. You saw that too, right?"

Seated in the passenger seat next to her, wide-eyed with her hands braced against the dashboard, Rae nodded an emphatic yes.

Hands still shaking, Sophia fumbled with her seat belt and struggled to stand on her quivering knees. Rae, too, got out, leaving her door open against the nearby guardrail. The car stereo blared a melancholy soundtrack as they crouched down by the beaming headlights, the rain falling like intermittent shooting stars through the shine.

"What do you think it was?" Rae asked, tracing her open palm along the car's bumper and grille.

"I have no idea," Sophia answered, turning on her toes to scan the illuminated trees for movement.

They both watched the swirling mercurial waves of a nearby pond, their eyes tracing the expanse of water before shifting to the water on the other side.

"But we saw it, right? It was real?" Rae asked, shivering.

"I think so."

If Sophia had to describe what she saw, she would say it was a snake, about as thick as a tree trunk, arching over Maine Route 11 like a low-hung rainbow. It poured itself from one part of the pond to the other. It was either brown or dark green, and it had a writhing accordion-like row of yellow spines rippling the length of its back.

Sophia returned to her door. "I don't care what it was, but either way, that's a nope rope for me."

She opened her door, but turning back, she discovered that Rae stood still with a finger raised in the air.

"I hear something," she whispered.

"Oh, come on!" Sophia whimpered. "Can we just go? Please? I've had a long day."

Rae looked back at her with a sly smile, guiding a bang of hair behind her ear.

"Okay, fine," Sophia said after a brief pause, resignation in her voice.

She reached in, removed the key from the ignition, and slammed the door shut. Stomping, she crossed behind the car to Rae's side, grabbed a notebook from the footwell, and shoved it into Rae's chest.

"What do you want to do?" Sophia asked, shrugging in surrender.

Standing statue still, Rae lifted her chin as if she had caught a scent and extended her hand to point to where the tree line neared the water.

"I think it went that way."

Sophia took out her phone. Waking up the screen, she saw that it only had two bars and no data. She turned the phone's flashlight on.

"All right, let's go. But let's make it quick."

She passed Rae as she climbed over the rail and slid down the mud-slicked slope toward a dual set of telephone poles. A breeze blew, and Sophia caught the flint-laced smell of smoke. She braced her hand on the first pole, then turned back to Rae.

Rae was standing on the shin-high, rusted silver guardrail, holding the notebook open above her head. A gold-dusted mist floated above, casting an amber glow across her face. Rae clapped the pages shut, sending sparks like a poked fire as she captured it like a firefly in a jar.

"You coming?" Sophia called.

"Yes, sorry," Rae replied, jumping down from the rail, the edges of the notebook's pages still prickling with light.

Sophia stepped up an incline, brush tugging on her jeans. She made it to the pine tree wall. Checking the road once more to see if Rae was still with her, she closed her eyes and, extending her hands, pushed through.

The canopy of trees above was like a cathedral ceiling, and the soft, springy roughage of the forest floor a carpet. Mosquitoes bounced at her face, and as she swiped at them, her hands pushed away the swarming insects, trailing swirling gold bursts that resembled the spidery shadows of spent fireworks. They drifted, bursting into a yellow shimmer.

Rae spun Sophia's shoulder a little as she leaped forward with the notebook. With a downward stroke, she swiped the shimmer from the air and cradled the notebook between her hands and elbows, giggling. The new glow on the pages underlit their faces, causing Sophia to smile as well.

Rae knelt to nestle the open notebook on a pile of dry leaves, then rose back up and extended her arms like growing vines. To Sophia's surprise and slight embarrassment, Rae started to dance.

She pirouetted an ever-expanding circle as the page's glow grew into translucent golden tentacles. The warm light bathed the nearby trees, whose trunks were like flaky batches of broken brownies with sticky golden sap seeping from between.

Sophia gasped as honeyed golden forms began to unfold midair, like crumpled pieces of poetry smoothing themselves out to join in Rae's dance.

A long-beaked bird appeared from between the trees, its pale yellow, crinkled paper-like wings glowing as it swooped in small circles. Rae rolled her hand, and the bird soared into line behind her, mimicking a loon's bubbling and puffing up in its throat.

Like a conductor, Rae pointed to a nearby branch, and unraveling through the needles came a small pot-bellied furry creature with a wizard's beard. To listen to the bird's song, it extended a small, outstretched hand to one of its bunny ears. The creature squeaked with joy and shook like a chattering squirrel. Rae waved, and it leaped down to stomp and move its dancing arms in front of the notebook's glow.

The glowing amber eyes of dozens more pierced the shadowy depths like tiny torn staple holes just beyond the notebook's reach. In the darkness, they circled Sophia and Rae, mirroring the dance. Rae willed the glow to become brighter, smiling for them to come closer.

An agonizing moaning bleat, rugged at the edges like an overstrained chainsaw, vibrated through the branches. The deep vibration pressed against their skin, and all of creation stopped. Sophia's head pivoted as golden orbs appeared, bursting to life like oven burners, forming a path toward the sound.

She turned back to Rae and caught the last starbursts of light as the bird and the squeaker leaped into the pages, and Rae closed the notebook.

"Should we?" Sophia whispered.

Another vibrating, guttural groan echoed as Rae nodded yes. She crouched to pick up the notebook.

Sophia followed the wisps as Rae trailed behind her, scooping up the small flames with the notebook. A loud ka-thoom, like the splash of a large rock hitting the lake bottom, directed their eyes up and through the spread fingers of another pine tree wall.

Through the needles, two giants wrestled in the depths of the nearby pond, the moon's reflection ringing around them. Sophia gazed at a towering albino moose with rippling muscles beneath its furry hide. It strained, shooting long clouds of breath from its snout as it bellowed and strained against the serpent they had seen earlier. The serpent's yellow-accented scales created a hypnotic flipbook effect as it curled around the moose's body.

Rae inched closer, while Sophia extended her hand, brushing against Rae's elbow.

"Rae, no. Stop. You can't go that far."

Rae evaded her fingertips and stepped into the pond's water.

"Rae, what are you doing? Get back here." Sophia gripped a nearby root tightly, afraid to extend her other hand out further.

Rae waded into the pond and held the notebook up and over her head, opening the pages.

A golden light swept through the night like a lighthouse beacon. Both giants stopped and stared. Sophia's heart pounded, and her temples begged for relief.

"Hey!" a man called from behind the tree line. "Hey! Are you okay?"

Sophia shook her head as reality snapped crisp and cold. She turned to look at him, raising a hand to block his flashlight.

"I saw your car on the side of the road, and, uh," he lowered the flashlight beam. "Rae? Is that your name? Are you okay?"

Sophia glanced at her hand and saw "Rae" written in marker on the notebook cover. She directed her gaze back to the water, and all was still except for the buzz of mosquitoes and the chorus of crickets.

"Hey! Want me to call you an ambulance?" He stepped forward into the clearing, slipping a little on the slope. "Whoa, kind of muddy, don't you think? Did you fall? Are you hurt?"

"No, I'm fine," Sophia said, turning back toward him.

He extended his hand to her. Above his head, like the twirling debris of a lit and burning sparkler in a child's hand, the looping letters came together.

"Tu seras voyant," Sophia whispered, taking his hand into hers. The letters faded.

"I'm sorry, what was that?" he asked, gently pulling her from the water.

"I said," she replied, holding the notebook tightly, "my name is Rae."

Shadowlight
Moe Moeller

The old woman nodded her gaily kerchiefed bald head to my question, but she didn't answer, so I tried again, "Great-grand-maman, tell me about the time you lived in the forest, up by Jackman near the lumber camp."

I scanned her deeply lined face, hoping to read some expression, but she could look stubbornly opaque, and not just because her eyes were clouded and effectively blind. My father, her grandson (a grandfather in his own right), says that for years, he has been watching her curl in on herself, like a leaf shed from the tree shriveling on the forest floor. We never knew her age for certain, something around a hundred. Now, as I listen to the recordings I made during her final weeks in the nursing home, I see her next to me, a shrunken figure in an overstuffed chair with a time traveler's confidence to slip easily through the past and present.

"Great-grand-maman, can you hear me?"

"I hear you just fine." Her voice rasps across the words. "You asked about the time I lived in the North Woods. That was more than a time—it was my childhood, over fourteen years." She gives out a cackle that dies as a cough. "Why do you care?"

"Our family wants to preserve your memories."

She grunts and lifts one hand as a dismissive flick. "What makes you think my memories are worth preserving?"

"Your memories are all we have of that time." I almost blurt out, "Soon, all we *will* have." The nursing home has been telling us for weeks that she's dying of multiple organ failures. I came to make recordings to let her life in the North Woods live on, at least as a family legacy.

"Tell me about your parents."

"My papa was born to a woman who worked in the lumber camp near Jackman when there were still hundred-foot white pines to harvest. My mama was an orphan abandoned by a kitchen worker. They were camp trash, never married, legal-like, but they were in love. They built themselves a cabin near a brook that empties into the Moose River. It took all day for Papa to walk to the trading store on the Old Canada Road and back."

"Are you their only child?"

"The only one I know of." Another cackle. She might be shriveling away, but she still has a sense of humor.

We laugh, and I offer, "It must have been a hard life. Such long winters."

"Hard? I didn't know it then. Not when you don't know how others live. My papa hunted and trapped, traded for the little that we needed from the outside world. There was game meat in the winter, fish in the summer, and smoked meat and grainy bread, greens in the springtime." She pauses to work her gums around something. "The winters were cold, sixteen hours of dark. We were used to it and weren't afraid of the dark. Nothing stopped us from making the rounds of his traps. It's something I still miss, the quiet of a winter's night with no sound but your breaths and the wind in the trees."

"Weren't you afraid living in the wild so far from other people?"

"It was people we were afraid of. I was about twelve when I began to understand that we were squatters. Everything was changing. Abandoned cabins became hunting lodges. Hunting lodges became crossroad villages. Someone built a school, a church, a post office. People got together to elect a sheriff."

I nod. "I know, it's still changing."

"Then we couldn't move fast enough to stay ahead of those men who demanded he stop illegal hunting and trapping. They made us leave whatever camp we holed up in. 'Course, it was squatting. The winter I turned fourteen, my parents gave me to an aunt who lived in Jackman. Well, they called her Aunt—Aunt Lucy. Later, I found she was just the childless wife of the storekeeper. She gave them money. They went out west. Idaho, I think. Never heard from them again."

"Nothing?"

"Neither could read or write. I only learned myself as a teenager. Only after Aunt Lucy managed to teach me the basics. Then, she wanted to send me to a boarding school in the fall. But I was still wild under my petticoats. For a whole summer, I planned my escape."

"You were a child. Where were you going?"

"To freedom." Her voice chirps the word, then lowers as if we were co-conspirators. "When everyone was asleep, I'd sneak downstairs into their store and steal supplies—blankets, tins of food, ropes, an axe, a knife. There was a trail I had marked that led deep into the woods near a stream where we once lived. There was a big rock angling out of the ground like a lean-to. I made a shelter. I cut birch saplings and spruce branches for walls and a door. Each night, I brought whatever I could carry and was back in my bed before morning." She nods and smiles, seemingly pleased with her memory. "I was sure I would escape Aunt Lucy before the fall and live in my secret hideaway forever."

"I can't imagine a fourteen-year-old traveling through the forest at night."

"I can see by shadowlight."

"What? We need visible light to see."

"In the dark forest, there is enough light. You see the night critters—bear, coyote, fox, fisher, weasel—by how their shadows move. You see the night owl by how she crosses the sky between you and the stars."

At the time, I assumed she was talking about the thin light reflecting off the moon and light-colored surfaces on Earth. Or, it was a way of adapting to her blindness.

"So, did you manage to run away?"

She wags her head, a back-and-forth motion. I was never sure whether it meant yes or no. "One night in August, as I got close to the shelter, I saw the door was open. It smelled musty like a bear, so I climbed about eight feet up a tree. I broke off a branch to use as a weapon. The cracking sound made something move in the shelter, and out popped a dark, hairy head. I was so afraid I couldn't breathe. I'd grown up with stories of evil creatures in the forest, like the Agropelter. You heard about him?"

"No. Agro-what?"

"Agropelter. They say he's strong, hairy, ape-like, and lives in hollow trees. He hates loggers and preys on them. He can heave a branch a thousand feet and knock a lumberjack out cold. If other workers find the man in time, he'll have a bump on his head for a few days, but if not ..." She wags her head again. "Agropelter is why some people disappear in the forest. If that monster was in my shelter, I was in big trouble."

"But since you're here talking to me, I'm guessing ..." I do my best to swallow a chuckle.

"Laugh if you want to. I couldn't breathe. I started feeling dizzy and fell out of the tree. The arms that caught me weren't no hairy ape. He was just an old man, and he smelled as bad as rotten fish."

"Another squatter?"

"He called himself a hermit, a woodsman living off the forest. I called him a liar. A real woodsman wouldn't be stealing someone's supplies. I told him it was my land and my shelter. He laughed at me and said, 'Girly, we're all just visiting here. The lumber and paper companies own the land, and they make the rules.' He let me go. When I came back the next night, he was gone, and so were my supplies. I went home mad as an Agropelter. I would've cracked a branch over his head if I'd 'a found him."

"What did you do?"

She smacks her lips and sniffs. "I turned him in. I told my aunt and uncle I'd seen him stealing from the store and knew about where he might be in the forest. They sent the sheriff's men and found his hideout. Last I knew, he was in jail. That was the end of my freedom, too. In September, I had to go to that school in Augusta to be finished off as a lady."

"Dad says you met your husband there and later moved back to Jackman."

"We compromised on many things, but I stuck to one rule: to live near the North Woods, even if he had other jobs. I raised my children there. Raised them to know the wilderness." She opens both palms of papery skin as if to show me she's not hiding anything. "'Course we agreed to only hunt and fish in season, legal-like, and to only take what we could eat."

"You never met the Agropelter?"

She lifts her face to cackle like a crow. "I was a child who believed in stories, but I became a twentieth-century woman. I went from living in a squatter's cabin with no indoor plumbing to seeing men walk on the moon and computers in pockets." She points a chicken-bone finger my way. "Mind you, the old stories have their lessons. Not like today. Now, half of what you see and hear is just made up to get you to buy something." She shifts in her chair, trying to lean forward. "Oh, here's Amy coming to take me to dinner."

I turn around to see the nursing aide named Amy standing quietly in the doorway. "How'd you know it was me?" Amy says. "This isn't my usual shift."

My great-grand-maman answers, "I know you in the shadowlight."

She died three months later. I still have the five hours of recordings I made. I edited the best of them and put them on my Facebook page reserved for family. When I replay them, I'm sitting by her chair, leaning in, a fellow time traveler. Though she started reluctantly, she kept on telling stories, almost all about her childhood in the North Woods. Some of them are likely true. I asked her multiple times about her life as a wife, mother, and grandmother, but she glossed right over those years. I guess they weren't that exciting.

Every summer, I rent a lakefront cabin in the Jackman area. The Moose River valley and lakes are still here, as is the unending forest. The lumber companies and other large landowners of the North Woods continue their harvests while allowing us to enjoy a little piece of that heaven. As the freedom thief once said: we're all just visiting here.

And, I came to understand shadowlight. It was quite a thrill the first time it happened. After enjoying sundown on the porch, something soared overhead, a dark silhouette traveling across the diamond-spangled night sky, an owl with wings moving up and down in perfect silence. I followed her shape as she settled on a high branch and hooted once, then disappeared. Shadowlight is all about recognizing the shape of things that come.

"Great-grand-maman, are you ever afraid? Not knowing what will happen to you?"

"When I was a child. Children are often afraid."

"But not of the dark or the wilderness, you said that."

"No, not what I know, but I'm sure scared when a shadow moves in a way I can't understand."

"I know. Me, too."

We Are But Guests in This Space
Sarah Walker Caron

In the warm light of the morning sun, the desolate branches sparkle with remnants of last night's rain. The soft ground, moist with excess water that has formed small puddles and trail-obscuring pools, is a complex patchwork of needles, water, dirt, and leaves. I step gingerly, trying to keep to the trail and wondering if my very presence here is disturbing the pristine peace.

We are but guests in this space.

I keep going, moving forward in my destination-less walk, wanting to imprint every gnarled tree trunk extending upwards to the bluebird sky in my memory so that when I am no longer here, I can close my eyes and be transported back. But that's not how memories work—at least not mine—so I settle for a few haphazardly snapped images with my ever-present smartphone. Maybe I'll be able to find them between the photos of ramen bowls, cheeseboards, and my kids' events when I need something to ground me. Or maybe they will be lost in the labyrinth of images I take, hoping to remember something that was important in the moment.

My memory isn't bad. It's good even. But it takes more than a peace-bringing walk to make a permanent imprint.

The melodies of birdsong echo through the branches, a soundtrack that follows me as I stretch my legs wide to try to avoid the soft mud where the trail is moistest.

In the reflections on the smooth surface of the puddles, I can see the treetops meet the sky. It's transcendent. I wonder if after dark, the milky trails of stars and distant planets, bright in the dark sky, would reflect, too.

We are but guests in this space.

Ferns unfurl. Moss grows across a rock. The first flowers of spring emerge in a gravel pile at the edge of the forest.

I'm in all black, layers of clothes and protection against the world, as I walk, one gray sneaker in front of the other, through needles and leaves, puddles and mud. I've come to the forest to get out of my head but I am finding myself being pulled deeper and deeper into thoughts.

The prolonged whoosh of an airplane overhead, trailing a white cloud behind it, reminds me that while I am in nature, humans have claimed all its spaces as theirs. We are the aliens ravaging the planet. We are the very thing we fear, making movies to explore our deepest terrors about what's to come.

We don't need tentacles and mind control to thrust our thoughts into the lifeblood of the Earth, snarling, "Die! Die!" We won't come as a sudden deep freeze and blizzard that takes over the country, forcing people south. Our spacecraft is roaring engines on four wheels and clouds of emissions dispersing into the air that should be pristine.

The gnarled stump of a tree spreads from the ground, a cascade of fingers reaching out to the felled trunk that remains nearby. It was an unforgiving winter of high winds and angry storms, and this ancient tree was among the victims. If I had a saw, I could slide it through to count the rings and see how many lives it lived before the man-made problems of a changing climate came for it.

That tree is not alone. There are others, some in the forest, some still across the trail, some pulled to the side, some humanely cut away. One, two, five, ten, twenty—how many trees have to fall before we see that the problem isn't them but us?

We've brought the destabilization, the warming and weirdening of climate, the loss of native plants, and the destruction of invasive species. We are an invasive species. We are ruining everything.

We are but guests in this space.

I keep walking. I am part of the problem. I've driven here in my fuel-efficient SUV that still breathes fumes into the air. I'm wearing a pair of shoes that I bought years ago, but when they give out, the fabric pulling away from the sole and the comfort lost, I will dispose of them. How do you recycle sneakers anyway?

Deep in the forest, I have escaped the intrusive thoughts that sent me to the woods, but they've been replaced with this reality. We are killing the planet. Why can't we coexist? I remember the bumper stickers of my childhood, slapped onto cars that are now long dead and rotting in junkyards that proclaimed with a variety of symbols that people should coexist, but what about humans and the planet? Why have we waited this long to do something?

I sat rapt in a lecture hall twenty-four years ago as Al Gore spoke about his hopes for climate action and the inconvenient truth of what humans had done to the planet, but he lost the election that year. We lost that chance for change. How have we let things get this far?

I grew up beneath a hole in the ozone layer three and four decades ago, the warnings of air pollution and rising cases of asthma among children a daily reality in our newspapers. I have asthma. Are they related? Does the planet have asthma, too? Back then, in the light-polluted New York night sky, I marveled at the few stars that shined brighter than our hubris.

Here in Maine at night, we can still see that the world is far more vast than our small existence on this small planet. And yet, we continue to conquer, to go bigger and brighter, to wink out the whispers of more.

I keep moving, one foot in front of the other. I smell the dew, hear the birdsong, breathe the air, and see the life and death that inhabits this forest. I wonder where the animals have gone.

And I wonder if it's already too late.

Woods at Night
Alexandra S. D. Hinrichs

I can't explain it
why my rough rooted, long branched fear
    of the dark
has been sanded down smooth
    soft, hollow
when I step into moon shadowed woods;
why as night deepens
and lantern light might catch
    an eye's starfire glimmer
the wild unknown calls out
    home
        home
            home
and I recognize
    that voice.

Night Woods North
Patricia Smith Ranzoni

Deneb
*   *Vega*
summer triangle   *
  vesper spires
    meadow sweet
        night pollination
          evening primrose
            grasshopper graze
              cricket racket
                  pond smell
                    eye shine
                        feathers after fur
                              Altair

Ethereal

William Henry Forester

Under the roof of night in Maine's North Woods, the sky stretches wide and deep; there is a sense of the eternal. Stars scatter like spilled diamonds on velvet cloth, each light a silent testament to the vastness, the beauty, the infinite in the quiet of the sky. The air smells of pine and earth, cool and sharp, a reminder of the wilderness that breathes around, within, through.

Pine and fir, tall and stoic, whisper in the dark breeze. Their voices are not spoken, but the sounds of the world turning, the heartbeat of the forest. Above, the Milky Way pours across the sky, a river of light, ancient and ever-flowing. It speaks in a language without words, of connections that stretch back through time, linking everything to everything else, a cosmic web of being.

The night is alive, with the presence of life unseen. Forest creatures move in the darkness, their lives a mystery, their paths crossing ours in the unseen dance of the nocturnal. The moon, when it rises, casts everything in a silver hue, transforming the unfamiliar into something even more otherworldly, ethereal.

There is a quietude here that sinks into the soul, a peace that is almost tangible. The vast sky overhead, with its uncountable stars, reminds us of our own smallness, our own part in this vast, interconnected universe. Yet, in that smallness, we feel a sense of belonging, of being part of something larger, something beautiful, something profound. The limitations of the day, the confines of our own minds, seem to dissolve, leaving only the essence, the soul that connects to the stars, the sky, the trees, the air that whispers of the ancient and eternal.

We are invited to simply be, to witness the majestic tapestry of the night unfold, a perpetual reminder of the endless cycles of the universe, of life itself. In this place, under this sky, we find a reflection of our own inner worlds, vast and mysterious, waiting to be explored.

Night Moss
Michelle Menting

such glory is moss
as if breath were cloth
but oh so soft look closer
level and you see mini trees
oh sight of dirt's horizon
earth without sun's gloss
of deadfall leaves
of grasses so veined
towards stars towards
saturated soil of beings
oh, how can this world be

thimble pockets of breath
and that feeling so alive
place your eyes at the ground
      how it's like mini trees!
every miniature thing
smell this ditch of sand
feel this muck of heartbeats
limbs stretch towards moon
sighs mud-wounded
such closeness to green
full of so much ache?

About the Contributors

DANI BANNISTER is a romance author who is empty nesting in Midcoast Maine. She holds a bachelor's in theatre and a master's in literary education. When she's not on the stage, or the page, you'll find her curled up with a good book.

KERRY W. BERNARD is a dark fantasy author with a penchant for nature magic, armed scoundrels, and messy romances. Monsters inevitably dominate her stories, stemming from a childhood encounter with one. As a lifelong Mainer with a background in ecology, she shares the same reverence for the woods and sea as the heroine in her award-winning debut novel *Drained* (Champagne Book Group, 2023).

MATT BERNIER lives in Pittsfield, Maine, and works professionally as a civil and environmental engineer, restoring sea-run fish to Maine rivers through projects like dam removals. His poetry has previously appeared in the *Maine Sunday Telegram*'s "Deep Water" column and Maine Public's "Poems from Here." In 2023 he won the Maine Postmark Poetry Contest.

ALICE BOLSTRIDGE has more than a hundred publications of poems, stories, and essays in many literary magazines and anthologies, including the *Cimarron Review*, *Intricate Weave* (Iris Editions), *Passager*, *Nimrod*, *Maine in Print*, *Bangor Metro*, and *The Café Review*. She authored the chapbook *Chance & Choice* (Finishing Line Press, 2017). Under the pseudonym Moore Bowen, she won the 2013 Kenneth Patchen Award for Experimental Writing for *Oppression for the Heaven of It* (JEF Books, 2013). Other writing awards include the Passager Poet Award (1995) and the Maine Literary Award in short works for poetry (2005, 2011).

MONIQUE BOUCHARD is a storyteller living in Old Town, Maine. She has a special passion for nineteenth-century Maine, a time when Bangor was known as the lumber capital of the world. Inspired by this era, she operates Madame

History, a seasonal tour company that provides walking tours through downtown Bangor and historic Mount Hope Cemetery to area visitors.

SHERRY PINEAU BROWN's work has been published in the anthology *Heliotrope: French Heritage Women Create* (Rheta Press, 2015). In 2008, she was a finalist for the Maine Literary Awards short works competition in fiction. Born and raised in Maine, she taught high school and college English in Colorado and Maine and is currently a lecturer at Colby College. Sherry lives on a grass-fed beef farm in Benton, Maine, with her husband, daughter, two cats, a dog, a few chickens, and a herd of cattle.

SARAH CARLSON has published three books of poetry—*The Radiance of Change* (2018), *In the Currents of Quiet* (2020), and *Tender Light Softens: When the Deep Places Speak* (Golden Dragonfly Press, 2022)—each poem paired with a photograph from her outdoor adventures in Maine and other wild places. Her books combine her love of nature, her healing journey, and her years of working in the education field. meanderingsoftheheart.blogspot.com

SARAH WALKER CARON is a Pushcart-nominated essayist as well as a food writer and author whose recent books include (with Jody Revenson) *Harry Potter and Fantastic Beasts: Official Wizarding World Cookbook* (Insight Editions, 2024), *Disney Princess Tea Parties Cookbook* (Insight Kids, 2022), and *Classic Diners of Maine* (The History Press, 2020). Her work has appeared in *Farmer-ish*, the *Washington Post*, the *Boston Globe*, and *SheKnows*. Sarah was named columnist of the year by the Maine Press Association in 2015. She is a part-time faculty member at the University of Maine and Husson University, where she teaches journalism and blogging.

WILLIAM CARPENTER grew up in Waterville and returned to Maine in 1972 to help found the College of the Atlantic, where he taught literature and creative writing for fifty years. He won the AWP and Samuel French Morse prizes and has published three books of poetry and three novels, most recently *Silence* (Islandport Press, 2021). He visits the North Maine Woods in all seasons, especially Baxter State Park, the Penobscot River Trails, and the Katahdin Woods and Waters National Monument.

GARRETT CONOVER co-founded North Woods Ways, a canoe and snowshoe guiding service that operated in Maine, Quebec, and Labrador from 1980 to 2007. He is the author of *Beyond the Paddle: A Canoeist's Guide to Expedition Skills—Poling, Lining, Portaging, and Maneuvering through the Ice* (Tilbury House, 1990), co-authored (with Alexandra Conover Bennett) *The Snow Walker's Companion: Winter Trail Skills from the Far North* (McGraw-Hill, 1994), and has won four awards for his novella *Kristin's Wilderness: A Braided Trail* (Raven Productions, 2006). His latest work, *Sauna Magic* (Custom Museum Publishing, 2019), combines photography and text.

CHRIS DAVIS released her first book, *Worthy: The Memoir of an Ex-Mormon Lesbian* (Publish Your Purpose), in 2023, for which she just completed the audiobook recording. She is also published in the anthologies *I Spoke to You with Silence* (University of Utah Press, 2022) and *Rivers of Ink: Literary Reflections on the Penobscot* (12 Willows Press, 2023). Chris was raised in Bangor and spent her childhood summers at her family camp in Aroostook County. She delights in sharing personal memories of her childhood in Maine and continues to live contentedly in her home state. www.chrisdavisproud.com

CHERI DOMINA helped found the Great Pond Mountain Conservation Trust and served as its executive director for twelve years. Early in her Maine sojourn, she was a reporter/editor at the *Bucksport Enterprise*, where she met her longtime camping buddy, Kris Cook. Cheri and Kris—the Semi-Tough Broads—continue to hike and camp all over the North Woods, but Baxter State Park remains their favorite place.

RICK DOYLE, poet and playwright, is the managing attorney at a nonprofit providing civil legal representation to survivors of domestic violence. His poems have appeared in *Kaleidotrope* and *The Café Review*. He lives in Bucksport, Maine.

MICHAEL G. DUNN, born and raised in Medway, Maine, lives in Veazie. He is the co-host and co-creator of *Book Talk*, a monthly book-centered event that meets in the Fogler Library at the University of Maine. Recently published in the *Maine Policy Review*, Michael is working on a novel about a paranormal investigator.

KATHLEEN ELLIS's poetry collections include *Red Horses* (Northern Lights, 1991), (with R. W. Estela) *Narrow River to the North: Poems & Prose of the Penobscot Watershed* (Amapola Books, 2011), and *Body of Evidence*, which won the 2022 Grayson Books Poetry Contest. Her poems have appeared in *The Café Review, Rumors, Secrets, and Lies, A Dangerous New World: Maine Voices on the Climate Crisis* (Littoral Books, 2019), and *Rivers of Ink: Literary Reflections on the Penobscot* (12 Willows Press, 2023). Poetry from her manuscript "Dear Darwin" was set to music for a Parma Recordings CD, nominated for a 2015 Grammy Award. Kathleen teaches creative writing at the University of Maine and lives on Marsh Island in Orono.

WILLIAM HENRY FORESTER was born in the coastal town of Inverness, Scotland. As the son of a fisherman, his early life was intertwined with the sea, rocky cliffs, and ancient tales. His writing blends Scottish, Irish, and American elements, and he writes extensively about life in Maine, about living on the rugged Maine Coast, and about his native homeland of Scotland. He creates children's books with positive social values and writes poetry and prose. William's poetry has won numerous awards and accolades in both North America and Europe.

NERO FYLER will never be described by anyone who knows him as quiet. For this reason, along with a host of personal factors, he dreams of retreating to a skull-shaped fortress on an island off the Maine coast. Currently residing in Bangor, he struggles with meeting deadlines.

DEVIN GIFFORD is studying English and creative writing at Dartmouth College. She's originally from North Yarmouth, Maine, where she spends the summers with her family, her two dogs, and her black cat. When she's not writing, she enjoys knitting, reading, and wandering in the woods.

SUZANNE DEWITT HALL is the author of *The Language of Bodies* (Woodhall Press, 2022), *Where True Love Is: An Affirming Devotional for LGBTQI+ Christians and Their Allies* (DH Strategies, 2017), the *Living in Hope* series (2021, 2022), the *Path of Unlearning* series (2021, 2024), and the *Rumplepimple* adventures (DH Strategies, 2015, 2017). Suzanne's poetry has appeared in several anthologies, including *Rivers of Ink: Literary Reflections on the Penobscot* (12 Willows Press, 2023) and *Smashing Bricks 3* (Poetry Pub News, 2023).

NANCY J. HAYDEN has an MFA from the University of Southern Maine. She co-authored (with her husband) *Farming on the Wild Side: The Evolution of a Regenerative Organic Farm and Nursery* (Chelsea Green Publishing, 2019), about their three decades of farming in Vermont. A keen student of World War I, she published the short story collection *The Great Dark: Noir and Horror Stories of World War One* (Northwind Arts, 2018). Nancy lives in Waldoboro, Maine, and is working on a World War I novel.

ALEXANDRA S. D. HINRICHS is a poet and author of picture books, including *I Am Made of Mountains* (Charlesbridge, 2023), *The Lobster Lady* (Charlesbridge, 2023), *The Pocket Book* (Abrams Books for Young Readers, 2023), *The Traveling Camera* (Getty Publications, 2021), and *Thérèse Makes a Tapestry* (Getty Publications, 2016). Her books have won awards, including Maine's Lupine Award and Wisconsin's Outstanding Achievement Award. Alex is a librarian and has worked in school, public, and academic libraries. She currently works in a public library tucked in the woods in rural Maine. She volunteers as a co-assistant regional adviser to the Society of Children's Book Writers and Illustrators, New England, and serves on the board of directors for Island Readers and Writers. She lives in Bangor with her husband, three wild sons, and two tame cats.

ANNALIESE JAKIMIDES is a writer and mixed-media artist. Published in many journals, magazines, and anthologies, her prose and poetry have been nominated for the Pushcart Prize and Best of the Net as well as cited in national competitions by Maine poets laureate and winners of the American Book Award and the NAACP Image Award. She's been a finalist in multiple genres in multiple years for the Maine Literary Awards. Her work was broadcast on NPR's *This I Believe,* and included in both its anthology and CD recordings. She is the co-writer of the musical *Love Affair.* Annaliese's particular place in the North Woods is Mount Chase, where she lived off the land for decades, pumping water by hand, growing almost everything the family ate, and raising three children. Small pieces of this life were captured in literary fragments published in the weekly *Houlton Pioneer Times* under the visionary editor Doug Fletcher. www.annaliesejakimides.com

MICHELE KRIEGMAN has written and produced for ABC News, *Slate*, *Info Security Professional Magazine*, iVillage.com, Lilith, Maine Public, Nippon TV, parenting magazines, Tokyo Broadcasting, and TV Asahi, among others. Having worked in a second career as a cybersecurity professional for over fifteen years, Michele now devotes herself to writing full-time, winning a 2024 Rockower Award for Essay from the American Jewish Press Association. Her published novels include *Tapioca Fire* (2014), *Rock Memoir* (Reunion Land Press, 2021), *From a Desert City by the Sea* (Reunion Land Press, 2021), and *Finding Faith* (Reunion Land Press, 2021).

FAITH LANE, a poet, author, adventurer, librarian, researcher, and genealogist, resides in Downeast Maine. She is the author of *lighthouses of midcoast maine & tales of the folk who lived there* (2024), *toxic & tonic* (2021), *zen(ish)* (2020), *Rural Librarianship: From Surviving to Thriving* (2024), *Emery Orson Lane & Rose Mabel Haskell: The Story of the Lane Farm* (2024), *Descendants of Emery Orson Lane & Rose Mabel Haskell of Fayette, Maine* (2024), *Veleda's Vision* (2025)—all published by Faith Lane Books.

SHANE LAYMAN earned a bachelor's degree in English/creative writing from the University of Maine, Orono. He resides near Bangor with his family and enjoys writing scary stories at night. During the day, he works as a children's librarian.

CATHERINE J.S. LEE—fiction writer, poet, haiga artist, high-school educator, journalist, community radio DJ, library board president, and arts center board member—still finds time to chase clouds and sunsets with her digital cameras. The author of two award-winning collections, *Island Secrets: Stories from the Coast of Maine* (Sea Smoke Press, 2022) and *All That Remains: A Haiku Collection Inspired by a Maine Childhood* (Turtle Light Press, 2010; reprinted by Sea Smoke Press, 2017), Catherine is working on another collection, *A Place to Land: More Stories from the Coast of Maine*.

EMILY M. LEONARD, a devoted wife and mother of two sons, is also a two-time Appalachian Trail thru-hiker. She grew up in Maine and, with that, developed a love for the outdoors. When life's demands free her, Emily can be found with a pack strapped to her back, wandering but never lost, writing and crafting about her adventures, or sharing her stories with others.

J.D. MANKOWSKI is a career coach at Husson University. His career as an author began with the 2015 release of *The Silver Scepter* after he graduated from Rutgers University. Two of his short stories are also featured in the anthologies *Rivers of Ink: Literary Reflections on the Penobscot* (12 Willows Press, 2023) and *Grifty Shades of Fey* (Fiction Vortex, 2020). J.D. lives with his wife and three cats in Veazie. www.jdmankowski.store

TODD MCKINLEY holds a doctorate in literacy education from the University of Maine. He shares his passion for writing with colleagues in the Maine Writing Project, at conferences, and at summer writing retreats while advocating for literacy education through his role as vice president for the Maine Council for English Language Arts. For more than a decade, he has also served as the accuracy judge for Maine's "Poetry Out Loud" competitions. He has been writing poetry for many years, publishing his work in *Maine Writes* and *Off the Coast*. Todd recently moved to southern Maine, where he spends much more time near the ocean while continuing his work as a middle-level educator.

MICHELLE MENTING teaches creative writing and poetry at the University of Southern Maine and directs the Gibbs Library in Washington, Maine. She lives in Whitefield, Maine. www.michellementing.com

MOE MOELLER is the author of four books in the *Pyke Island Mystery Series* set in Downeast Maine (all forthcoming by 12 Willows Press). She also writes short stories and poetry for anthologies and plays for local community theaters. In 2024 two of her ten-minute plays were performed during a short-play festival in Lamoine, Maine.

CHRISTOPHER PACKARD is a science teacher, folklorist, and storyteller based in the greater Bangor area. He is the assistant director of the International Cryptozoology Museum and the author of *Mythical Creatures of Maine: Fantastic Beasts from Legend and Folklore* (Down East Books, 2021) and the children's book *Lumpy's Gift* (12 Willows Press, 2023). www.christopherpackard.com

BRUCE PRATT is the author of the poetry collection *Boreal* (Antrim House, 2007), the novel *The Serpents of Blissfull* (Mountain State Press, 2011), *The Trash Detail: Stories* (New Rivers Press, 2018), and the poetry chapbook *Forms and Shades* (Clare Songbirds Publishing House, 2019). His writings have appeared in several dozen magazines, reviews, and journals in the United States, Canada, Ireland, and Wales. Bruce edits the journal *American Fiction*.

PATRICIA SMITH RANZONI grew up in outback Bucksport, where she is the town's poet laureate. Her work has been widely published, most recently in *Still Mill: Poems, Stories & Songs of Making Paper in Bucksport, Maine, 1930–2014* (2017) and *Rivers of Ink: Literary Reflections on the Penobscot* (12 Willows Press, 2023).

AMY RAY is a visual artist and poet from Eastport, Maine. She earned a master's of fine art at Brooklyn College. She has shown her paintings, collages, and drawings extensively throughout Maine and beyond. She is currently working on a book of poetry, poetic prose, and a body of textile artworks.

LEE SANDS is a mother, poet, and literacy aide who was born and raised in Maine and calls the North Woods home.

NOMAR SLEVIK is an independent creator, writer, researcher, and investigator in numerous aspects of the paranormal. He delights in sharing stories through different mediums, including books, documentaries, and podcasts. He has been fascinated by all things paranormal since childhood, beginning with a UFO encounter when he was four years old. Nomar's lifelong passion has been to research, investigate, write, and share otherworldly encounters, presenting them in a way that highlights the human element in profoundly strange encounters.

RET TALBOT is an award-winning independent journalist, science writer, and author. His work has appeared in *National Geographic*, *Discover*, *Yale Environment 360*, and *Mongabay*, among other outlets. At home in the field with scientists, his books include (coauthored) *Banggai Cardinalfish: A Guide to Captive Care, Breeding & Natural History* (Reef to Rainforest Media, 2013), the story of a scientific expedition to Sulawesi to uncover a mystery surrounding an endangered reef fish, and *Chasing Shadows: My Life Tracking the Great White Shark* (William Morrow, 2023), a conservation success story about the restoration of the white shark to northwest Atlantic. He lives and writes in Rockland, Maine, with his wife, scientific illustrator Karen Talbot, and the most amazing flock of ducks.

GREG WESTRICH, a writing and literature teacher at Deer Isle/Stonington High School, spent his adult life wandering around the country having adventures before settling in Maine. Besides publishing a dozen hiking guides with Falcon, he has published many articles in newspapers and magazines, including *Down East Magazine, Canoe and Kayaking*, and *Bird Watching*. He also regularly gives talks and slideshows at libraries and nature-based clubs. www.gregwestrich.com

Index - Contributors

Index - Selections

Fiction

Nonfiction

Poetry